PENGUIN BOOKS

MOON OVER MINNEAPOLIS

Fay Weldon was born in England, reared in New Zealand, and educated in Scotland, where she took a degree in economics and psychology. After a decade of odd jobs and hard times she started writing, and now is well known as a novelist and screenwriter. Her novels include *The Cloning of Joanna May*, *The Hearts and Lives of Men*, *The Life and Loves of a She-Devil*, *Darcy's Utopia*, and *Life Force*, and are translated the world over. She is married with four children and divides her time between London and Somerset.

FAY WELDON

MOON OVER MINNEAPOLIS

PENGUIN BOOKS

PENGUIN BOOKS
Published by the Penguin Group
Viking Penguin, a division of Penguin Books USA Inc.,
375 Hudson Street, New York, New York 10014, U.S.A.
Penguin Books Ltd, 27 Wrights Lane,
London W8 5TZ, England
Penguin Books Australia Ltd, Ringwood,
Victoria, Australia
Penguin Books Canada Ltd, 10 Alcorn Avenue, Suite 300,
Toronto, Ontario, Canada M4V 3B2
Penguin Books (N.Z.) Ltd, 182–190 Wairau Road,
Auckland 10, New Zealand

Penguin Books Ltd, Registered Offices:
Harmondsworth, Middlesex, England

First published in Great Britain by
HarperCollins Publishers Ltd 1991
Published in Penguin Books 1992

1   3   5   7   9   10   8   6   4   2

PUBLISHER'S NOTE
These stories are works of fiction. Names, characters, places, and incidents either are the
product of the author's imagination or are used fictitiously, and any resemblance to actual
persons, living or dead, events, or locales is entirely coincidental.

Page 181 constitutes an extension of this copyright page.

LIBRARY OF CONGRESS CATALOGING IN PUBLICATION DATA
Weldon, Fay.
Moon over Minneapolis / Fay Weldon.
p.   cm.
"First published in Great Britain by HarperCollins Publishers Ltd.
1991"—T.p. verso.
ISBN 0 14 01.4542 7
I. Title.
PR6073.E374M66   1992
823'.914—dc20   91–27004

Printed in the United States of America

Contents

STORIES OF WORKING LIFE

Subject to Diary

If you do nothing unexpected, nothing unexpected happens.

Oriole Green gave her name to the clinic receptionist, an unsmiling girl with dark skin and blonde hair and almost no eyebrows at all, who punched Oriole's name up on the computer and then asked her if she'd been to the clinic before. Oriole said yes, without thinking, for she was under considerable stress, and the girl with no eyebrows punched some more buttons and then said flatly, 'You're lying. You haven't.'

Oriole was on the eve of her fortieth birthday and for fifteen years had been spoken to, on the whole, and at least out of the bedroom, with politeness and respect. Though in the bedroom, she had noticed, men who were most – no, reverential was the wrong word, as was courteous; guarded was perhaps more accurate – were the ones who most wished to take her down a peg or so: called her names, slapped her around a little. Oriole didn't mind: it was a relief. It was the price, she reckoned, a woman paid for being successful. Nothing was for nothing.

But this was not a bedroom. This was not a suitor, an impregnator, an erotic hit-and-runner, this was a chit of a fat-faced girl behind a desk in the Serena Clinic for Women, a double-fronted house in a dusty suburban garden where pregnancies were terminated for money, and such a girl, who was doubtless paid twice what her equivalent in the public sector would be, should not feel entitled to be rude to clients. The girl wore a pink name-tag on her white coat. It read 'Daisy'. Daisy should smile and be friendly and helpful; and out of human kindness, what's more, not merely in the interest of good public relations. Except, Oriole supposed, a girl in her early twenties who was not pregnant, who was not a supplicant for termination, would feel superior to her less fortunate sisters. Or perhaps, more likely, since the waiting list at the clinic was long, the problem was merely that no one had bothered properly to train the reception staff. Even in the private sector, termination came under the heading 'seller's market'.

'I must have made a mistake,' said Oriole, returning rudeness with courtesy, as one should. She had most certainly been to the Serena Clinic twice before, only, of course, as she would have remembered sooner had she not been under stress, using another name on each occasion. On her first visit, when she was 28, she had given her married name, and on the second, when she was 36, her boyfriend's surname, out of some kind of rivalry, she now supposed, with his wife. At the time she had just felt better using his name, not her own. But now she had given the clinic her own original name, her school and professional name: as if finally she accepted responsibility, not for a child exactly, but at least for the non-event the child must of necessity be: and she felt less somehow hole-in-corner, in fact rather open and brave.

Even 'child' sounded wrong. A putative non-child perhaps: an alleged and accidental non-child. Of course this non-child, this growing cluster of cells, had in a way to be congratulated, inasmuch as, so successfully and so far, it had evaded all the powerful suggestions that it should not be, should not come into existence, egg and sperm by some miracle of happenstance colliding and joining, the two amongst millions not to succumb to the hazards set up by nature itself – a too acid, too alkali womb: a too early, too late arrival of the egg and/or delivery of the sperm: and so forth; oh, well done, well done! Not to mention the more considered incentives towards not-to-be: the contraceptive poisons, the rubber sheaths, the hormone-induced non-receptivity, the other many traps and fail-safe devices invented by humanity to stop itself breeding itself out of existence. What, survived all this? Still living? And then, once fertilized, to have clung on satisfactorily; to have successfully set the welcoming mechanism of the host body into vigorous motion – oh yes, you had to congratulate this cluster of dividing cells, even as your own surging hormones sickened you.

Well done, well done, you had to say, for having got so far! But
also, so sorry, I do have to hit you on the head at this the last and
greatest hurdle. I don't want you. You can't survive if I don't
want you. You got it right, but in the wrong body. A factor beyond
your comprehension: one you were too tiny to comprehend, let
alone forestall. That the whole great intended unit should notice
you as you grew, and turn against you. For now that your scale
has changed other forces must come into play. Pipped at the post,
oh brave and courageous one, the one amongst millions. What
was the month now? June? Left to itself it would be born in
November.

'Funny thing to make a mistake about,' said Daisy uncheerily.
She had a hairy upper lip, and had bleached the dark hairs, which
was a mistake. Why didn't she just tweeze them out? 'Sit down,'
said fat-faced, greasy Daisy, as if Oriole's standing was in itself a
nuisance.

Oriole sat down. There was one other person in the waiting room,
which was painted pale pink and had pictures on the walls of pretty
ladies in crinolines, in silhouette. She was a thin girl with a white
face and red-rimmed eyes, who lowered her eyes to her copy of *House
and Garden* rather than meet Oriole's. There was an article inside the
magazine, Oriole knew, in the series 'Successful Women', featuring
Oriole Green. Oriole had cut it out and pinned it on her kitchen
wall. She was proud of it. The thin girl flicked past the page.

Oriole had been named for a bird, so her mother said: born to
soar and fly. Of course you succeed, said her mother, proudly.
Sometimes Oriole felt like a bird: she had a lean, small, muscly
body covered by the finest designer feathers, a small beaky nose
and bright sharp intelligent eyes, and a lot of reddish hair: she
could feel herself sometimes hopping about: this appointment, that
appointment, up those stairs, down that lift, pecking around, then
soaring, soaring –

There was an uncomfortable silence in the waiting room. The thin
girl snivelled, and lit up a cigarette.

Oriole took out her diary and looked through November. It was a busy month. Ex-King Alleyne of a minor Arab state had his book coming out: the Shrinks were making a come-back: there was the Head Office Conference in Reykjavik: all fourteen branches would be represented. She, Oriole Green, personnel manager, would be speaking. In December the company was going public. You had to prepare people for change, even if change was to their advantage people hated it; hers was to be the keynote speech. How could you fit in having a baby with all that, even if you wanted one, loved the father? Neither of which she did, not for lack of trying. How could you find a man to love; a man who was altogether admirable and superior to yourself, once you were past, say, thirty, and earning well? And you didn't have babies by, marry or set up home with men you didn't love. Did you? Others seemed to, it was true, but only women with no standards, no expectations, no subtlety.

Oriole couldn't remember waiting like this, on previous occasions. She'd been shown immediately to her room, undressed, settled down, been weighed up by the anaesthetist and gone straight into surgery. She felt obscurely that the wait was Daisy's fault.

Oriole flicked through the current week. She had managed to adjust her appointments to keep not only this afternoon free but tomorrow morning as well. Body and mind might need a little time to recover, to adjust to a change in state. She reckoned to feel low for a week or so in any case. The sooner the operation was done the better. Hours counted. This particular hour was somehow dripping uncontrolled out of her life, thanks to Daisy.

The pale girl and her suitcase were taken away by a nurse whose name-tag said 'Audrey'. Daisy and Audrey, the girls who worked at the clinic. Audrey smiled a great deal, showing broken teeth. Audrey's smile was worse than Daisy's unsmile. Were the Serena Clinic forward-looking, it would have had Audrey's teeth capped. Or not employed her at all. The sense of things rotten or bad or missing in such a place as this surely had at all costs to be avoided.

'Will it be long?' Oriole asked Daisy, rashly.

Daisy looked back at Oriole and thought unspeakable things or so it seemed to Oriole. Oriole was, quite determinedly, not looking her best. She wore no eye make-up. People went either way at funerals, she noticed. They either looked their best or their worst. 'Enjoy it while you can,' said Daisy.

Oriole had worn her best to her father's funeral: her worst to her mother's. She wondered why. She hadn't grieved over-much when either of them died; she thought perhaps because she loved them, and so felt little guilt, and their deaths were after all timely. Her father had gone suddenly, through a stroke. Her mother lingered on in a kind of passive shock for less than a year, then had cancer of the liver diagnosed, and died promptly and painlessly almost of her own volition. They'd been in their seventies, and neither had enjoyed it. They were accustomed to being active, and were not so short-sighted they couldn't see the litter on the floor, the bits of stick and wrappers that the dog chewed up, which they were now too stiff to bend to pick up; they had to wait for the daily help to arrive to see to it. Old age was no way to end a life. If you had a diary for a whole life, all the appointments would be crammed near the beginning: getting fewer and fewer as you flicked through, until the pages were all but empty.

Oriole felt tears in her eyes. She knew Daisy would misconstrue them. Daisy did. Daisy said, 'Sometimes people change their minds –' but she said it unpleasantly; judgementally, Oriole thought, she who had been named after a bird, to soar and sing and rejoice. The kind of women who end up in this waiting room of mine are feckless and hopeless, Daisy implied: the kind who change their minds and put me and my computer to endless trouble.

Oriole smiled coolly at Daisy and made no reply.

Oriole thought, well, this is really not time wasted. Thank you, Daisy. This is thinking time, reflective time. Everyone needs this quality time. In progressive businesses such spare time is built into timescales, just as free periods were when we were at school.

No doubt that particular free time was the result of timetabling inconsistencies and inadequacies. Never mind: we students, being ignorant, interpreted it as a gift, a kindness, from a benign authority and were the happier for it.

Seven weeks from her last period. She looked that up in her diary too. There was the little tick. Regular as clockwork; predictable as the moon. Was the moon predictable? She supposed so. The moon came and went, waxed and waned, without Oriole noticing. What was the point of noticing the moon, if the moon took no notice of you? 'Oriole,' her mother once said, 'life is not all give and take, tit for tat: you do this and I'll do that, watch my back and I'll watch yours. Other factors intervene.' But what? Love? Her mother loved her father and she, Oriole, had intervened by being born. And even love ended in death, in silence. In strokes and cancer of the liver.

So little time to think. Too tired to think when she got home: and for holidays she'd go to health hydros where she'd starve and exercise herself into somewhere between a stupor and a high. Too tired to talk. And who was there to talk to, even if you could formulate the right words to echo the bizarreness of your thoughts? By the time you'd said too often to too many friends, when they rang to suggest lunch, or an outing, or a holiday, 'Just a moment, I'll get out my diary,' and then, 'Sorry, I can't make it,' they'd lost patience, moved on, thought you valued something more than them. Which in a way you did, so you could hardly blame them. Men in business had wives to live their lives for them: remember birthdays, arrange dinners, have their children: Oriole only had herself. She'd been married once: but it hadn't outlasted a year. He'd been an air-traffic controller: he knew exactly where not only he but everything and everyone else would be, ought to be, at a certain time: in the end the uncertainty of her hours, the sudden crises, the middle-of-the-night phone calls – some of her clients were Australians, and just didn't seem to comprehend that their glorious midday was someone else's exhausted two in the morning – had defeated him. 'We're heading for a crash,' he'd said, panicky, and so of course they were. He wanted her to be at home when he was, waiting, coming into existence when he opened the front door, blanking out of it when he left. Well, of course, she wanted him to be the same. There when she wanted him: not when she didn't. Francis, her husband.

She'd felt bad about failing to meet his demands, and confused by his expectations. She couldn't concentrate, she'd quite forgotten to look in her diary. Francis had been the one to point out that she hadn't bled for two months. She was three months gone by the time she got to the Serena Clinic. That had been really horrible. And when she got back four days later there were two significant messages on the answerphone: one on Monday asking her to be a fill-in speaker at the Toronto conference – and she knew her promotion depended upon it – and one on Wednesday from Francis saying he knew she would go to Toronto, not stay at home, and so he was going off himself. Where? Anywhere, just somewhere else, away from her. And so he had. Now he was married to a nice boring little stay-at-home and had two children. The elder one had been born with some disorder which made its head swell up with water – Oriole somehow felt it was her fault, though of course that was absurd. But she'd been upset. She'd loved him, this man who had the flying machines within his care and control – this dextrous male. If he'd given her time she could have broken the addiction, because that was what it was, an addiction to her diary. Subject to diary. The diary that kept you forgetful, so busy you were being reminded. Forgetful of what?

She couldn't remember now why she'd felt obliged to get rid of the air controller's baby. Some necessity, some need, some fear? Perhaps his. Or had she just been putting motherhood off to some more convenient time? If that had been the reason, she'd been wise enough. If she looked through past diaries it was clear there never had been, never would be, a convenient time.

Speaking the unspeakable. Daisy was punching up names and numbers on her computer. She could say to her, 'Daisy' – such an advantage to the anonymous, the habit of putting name-tags on the humble – 'Daisy, why do you pluck out your eyebrows but leave your lip-hairs alone? Shouldn't it be the other way round?' But you couldn't say that. Not just because Daisy could pull a string or two, make sure Oriole's anaesthetic was too light, expose her to the risk of septicaemia and other foreseeable things as well – the humble had all kinds of amazing powers – but because it was not done to say things to people which would hurt in the short term though help in the long. A pity. She searched for something friendly and companionable to say to Daisy, but failed.

What could she say? 'I am an important person; please treat me with courtesy'? No. Any woman with her legs apart and some tearing, rending instrument up inside her as she slapped nature in the face was pretty much of a muchness with the last one on the table, the next one to come.

'You are here on the computer,' said Daisy, 'if Green's your maiden name?'
'Yes,' said Oriole. Maiden name. How sweet and naive it sounded. She wondered what kind of girl she'd been. How could one ever know: you could only see yourself from the inside out. She thought she probably hadn't ever had much brain, only competence and a kind of soaring sensuality. So how had it gone wrong? Was it mood, a kind of generalized feeling tone, or nature, or just the chance events of a certain day which had led her to this point: forty, childless, unmarried. Not a bad point to be. Nothing wrong with being forty, or childless, or unmarried, except that spoken all together they sounded too final, too unwanted for comfort.

'The first time you were here you let it go three months,' observed Daisy, 'and there were complications. Still, it hasn't affected your fertility.'
'Clearly not,' said Oriole. The second time she'd been only six weeks' pregnant: that was Hassan's baby. She remembered well enough why she'd let that one go by. Hassan had been beautiful, beautiful, but married: he didn't think, or reason, or plan: he couldn't organize anything: he was a gardener: he loved all living, growing things except, it seemed, Oriole's baby. She didn't want to lose him so she'd lost the baby instead: she never even told him. She lost him anyway. He worked for the Parks Department, nine to five, and the complications of her unsocial hours and his getting

away in secret from his wife had quite worn out the romance. Lovers looked silly in diaries: their initials softly pencilled in. 'I will meet you, my darling, my darling, subject to diary!' Men could do it: women couldn't: that was the problem.

'An expensive form of contraception, if you ask me,' said Daisy. 'I didn't ask you,' said Oriole.

She could see this was her last chance. But how did you have a baby by your PA and go on working in the same office with him? Stop work and live off what? With him? Off him? On his lower salary? He wouldn't get much further up the ladder: she wrote his annual report: she knew it well enough. Oriole Green, a source of scandal and mirth! Oriole? Oh, Oriole the high-flyer: flew over a volcano, got her wings burned, plummeted, died. Babies got into your heart and twisted knives of guilt and obligation. Babies killed you: everything in you that wasn't totally female, at any rate. That flourished, to the detriment of the whole.
'Sorry I spoke. No need to snap,' said Daisy. 'Everyone snaps in here. It's the stress.'

And what you knew you grew to need, couldn't do without. The luxury of her bedroom: with its view over the city: the sense that it honoured you, found you special: the routine of early morning: the private, leisured silk, carefully chosen, against the skin: the softness of pale carpet; again yet softer, paler feet as you searched with your toe for your slipper, warm and safe inside while wind and rain and nature pattered against the pane. She didn't want to give it up. Other people, men, babies, intruded into the eroticism of solitude. Perhaps you had to get married before you were twenty, have babies before you were twenty-five, before you knew what there was to miss.

'Are you really nearly forty?' asked Daisy, looking across from her computer screen, 'because you don't look it.' Oriole smiled coldly; perhaps this impossible Daisy was a temp: filling in for someone who must surely know how to behave, and understood without being told that the personal information now freely available about everything and everyone to any girl with a computer at her fingertips had somehow, in the interests of the social niceties, to be referred to but at the same time tactfully overlooked.

'Mind you,' said Daisy, 'we get people in here up to fifty, but mostly they've got six already and it's medical. Lots of women have babies at forty.'

'More fool them,' said Oriole shortly: she would have stayed silent if it weren't for the sudden flow of words from Daisy's hairy mouth which filled the pale-pink room in a dangerous way, and might break the silence for ever if they were not somehow stilled. It didn't work.

'There are tests for Down's Syndrome,' went on Daisy, 'if that's what you're worrying about.'

'I hadn't even considered it,' said Oriole. Nor had she. A non-child cannot have Down's Syndrome or, if it does, can hardly suffer from feelings of inadequacy on that account; not during its brief putative existence.

'Lots do,' said Daisy. 'You'd be surprised. It isn't a nice job, this: but if I don't do it someone worse will.'

'It seems perfectly reasonable work to me,' said Oriole. 'I imagine there is a high degree of job satisfaction. You're working in the community, with people, in a healing environment, meeting very important human needs.'

'Is that what I'm doing?' asked Daisy. 'It seems to me I'm working for a crew of murderers and not even getting danger money.'

'What sort of danger?' asked Oriole, startled.

'Being hated,' said Daisy. 'People just sit where you're sitting, waiting, beaming out their dislike.'

'Perhaps it comes from the babies,' said Oriole, before she had time to think. 'Perhaps the hostility comes from them. They can hardly thank you for what you're doing. Well, not doing. But for helping organize the doing. That is to say the doing-away-with.'

'Oh thank you,' said Daisy. 'That's a real help. Ta very much.'

She swung her swivel chair so that her back was to Oriole. Her hair was greasy. There was a yellowy stain down the back of her white coat.

Oriole thought, this is me, Oriole Green, sitting in a female clinic having a spat with a greasy girl at a computer. This is where love leads you: or sex, while it lasts. And of course it wouldn't last, couldn't. The gap between affairs lengthened: she noticed it. Once one lover trod hard upon the heels of the last: now years could intervene: the diary of love had long, long stretches of nothingness. Last chance, last chance. She might still find someone like herself, intolerably busy, to settle down with, subject to diary, to provide a baby with a proper home but, come to think of it, she doubted it. Last chance!

'Daisy,' said Oriole, 'there's a yellowy stain down the back of your overall. I only mention it because you can't see it, and I expect your employers put quite a price on smartness.'

'They put a price on murder,' said Daisy, 'Nothing else. I could wear a butcher's overall for all they cared. Bloodstains and all. How much are they asking you, Oriole?' She consulted the screen. 'Eight hundred and twelve pounds plus anaesthetic fees. Wow! Of course, you are forty. That puts the insurance premiums up. Most women get out at about six hundred. No reduction for quantity, it seems, or you'd be less. And the stains down the back of my overall will be baby sick. And my own view is if you have a baby you should stay home and look after it, but chance would be a fine thing, wouldn't it?'

'Chance,' said Oriole, wings healed, spirits soaring, 'is a very, very fine thing,' and when the smiling nurse with broken teeth came in to take her and her overnight suitcase up to her room, she said she'd changed her mind.

'You'll lose your deposit,' said the nurse, her smile simply blanking out, not even fading. 'Your room being booked, and the operating theatre too. We can't rebook at this late stage. These last-minute changes of mind are very inconsiderate of others. And we've had a whole spate of them lately.' The nurse looked very hard at Daisy, knowing perfectly well whose fault it was, but Daisy had fallen sullen and silent again and didn't so much as raise her eyes from the screen.

As for Oriole, she asked for a year's leave of absence on full pay and got it, with no argument from anyone. If you do the unexpected, unexpected things happen.

I Do What I Can and
I Am What I Am

There is a dragon tattoo on the back of Romula's left hand, for all the world to see, and engraved in her heart (as *Calais* was, they say, in Queen Mary's) is the phrase *'I do what I can and I am what I am'*. In Romula's mind dragon and words are interconnected. A tattoo's there for life, and that's that, and Romula doesn't mind one bit, so long as the phrase stays too.

I do what I can and I am what I am.

Let me tell you more about Romula. Last year she won the Miss Skyways Competition. She won against 82 other girls, all cabin crew – air hostesses, as we used to say – on International Skyways. She deserved to win: not just because she was pretty, and smart, and efficient, and friendly, and everyone liked her, but because she loved her job: it never ceased to thrill her: to fly the Airways of the World, to be the girl in the ad: to watch the mountains moving by below, the plains unfolding: sometimes she would catch her breath with the pleasure of it all. It was her gift, never to be blasé. Romula, years into her job, would still look out of the aircraft window on a clear day, when there was nothing else to do – which was not often, granted – and marvel at the miracle of flying. She would go forward into the cockpit with the crew's food – different dishes for everyone, in case of food poisoning – and watch their strong male hands move amongst the instruments, and rejoice at the luck which got her to this place, this point of time, this source of power, this wonderment.

'You *what?*' demanded Liz her mother. 'You won *what? Miss Skyways?* For God's sake keep quiet about it.'

Liz Ellis was a hard-working, hard-drinking, high-thinking feminist. She hadn't worn a skirt since she was pregnant with Romula, and that was twenty-four years ago. She'd stopped Romula playing with dolls, slapped her if she dusted, tried to give her a proper education so she could take a meaningful place in society, and look what happened. *Miss Skyways.* Handing out G and Ts to businessmen. What sort of life was that?

Sometimes, when Romula went forward to the cockpit, she'd catch the eye of the pilot, or the first officer. Of course she did. How could she not? Hotels in far-off places can be lonely: the camaraderie of the air is strong: tension and danger demand relief: excitement smoulders in the sky as well as on the earth: like salt on meat, passing sex brings out the full flavour of a rich life. Sometimes the sex trembled on the edge of love; never quite, for Romula.

I do what I can and I am what I am.

Men would take Romula's small hand, hold it, pass a finger over the lines of the blue, curling, disfiguring dragon and say, 'How did you come by that? What happened?' But she never told them. She told me, though, when I met her at breakfast in Singapore, so I'm telling you. Should you come across her, when you travel Skyways, should the little lace half-glove on the hand of the girl who brings your coffee, tongs out the hot towels (Club Class only), slip back to reveal the macho stamp of the dragon, please keep it to yourself. I wouldn't want her to think a confidence had been betrayed. Details have of course been altered to protect her identity. And in a way it is everyone's story: everyone, that is, who doesn't do what their mother wants.

I do what I can and I am what I am.

When she was fourteen, Romula had the prettiest hands: soft but not puffy, delicate but not feeble, slender fingers just right for rings

– not so short they looked stubby, not so long they seemed to have
a life of their own and were scary, as fingers can be; her nails
were healthily pink and almond-shaped: the skin of the hand
translucently white – but then she was a natural blonde: blue veins
made a faint tracery beneath the skin, and the ones on the
back of her hand travelled straight to her heart, she knew they
did.

'Romy, stop waving your hands about and get on with your
homework! The way out of all this is education.' Liz's hands were
big, square and rough: they were competent: they made you feel
safe: only once had Romy's father raised his fist to Liz and Romy
– that was when Romy was three – and Liz had pushed him out
the door for ever.

'We'll manage on our own,' she said. 'No man's better than half
a man,' and presently she was standing on platforms waving her
own big, effective hands about, speaking on the rights of women,
while little Romula stood somewhere apart, standing on first one
foot, then another.

'When I grow up,' said Romula at five, 'I'm going to be a nurse.'
'No, you're not,' said Liz and all her many female friends in
chorus. 'You're going to be a doctor.'

Romula thought that was a perfectly horrid idea and took off her
dungarees and borrowed one of Sylvie's party dresses (Sylvie lived
next door and Liz wished she didn't) and went straight out and
played in the garden like that. She wasn't often so naughty, though.
She cried afterwards and told Liz she didn't know why she did it,
and it was true, she didn't.

I do what I can but I'm not what I am.

When Romula was crossed in love or unhappy in any way she'd
develop a little wart where the top of her thumb rubbed against
her forefinger. When she was in love again, happy again, it went
away. Men looked at Romula's hands a lot, in a speculative way,
which at first vaguely alarmed her. Other girls had legs which got
looked at, or necks, or breasts, or eyes – it was Romula's hands
which mesmerized, promised, enchanted.

That was what women did to men, Romula believed, at sixteen. Mesmerized, promised, enchanted. Then they married you and you lived happily ever after. She told her mother so.

'What are you *talking* about?' shrieked her mother. 'Dear God, what am I going to do with you?'

Romula was struggling with physics, chemistry, biology: her mother had to fight the school's obstinacy, stupidity and sexism to achieve it. And she had. Liz always got what she wanted. Romula was to be a doctor. The pressure of the pen raised a blister on Romula's middle finger. The blister went septic. She couldn't work for months, it hurt so; she failed exams.

I try but I can't and I'm not what I am.

When she was sixteen, a fortune-teller read Romula's palm. 'What pretty hands,' she said. Well, everyone said that. But then she said – 'You'll grow up to break your mother's heart. See there, the gap between the head line and the life line, where they rise. That's good for the child, bad for the parent. Unbiddable!'

Yet Romula was the sweetest, gentlest thing. Not a scrap of her father in her, that roistering, fornicating, loud-mouthed bully. Liz missed Romula's dad, for all she claimed she didn't. Romula knew it. But when men go, women must make do, and Liz had her pride. Everyone makes a virtue of necessity.

When she was seventeen Romula said to Liz, 'I'm going to the fair with Sylvie.' Sylvie was still living next door. Sylvie giggled a lot. She had little red raw knuckly hands which were never quiet: 'Like her mouth,' said Liz. Sylvie had left school: now she did nothing in particular. She wore very short skirts and her hair was yellow-blonde, not natural blonde, like Romula's.

'Why do you have to go with Sylvie?' asked Liz. 'Come to that, why do you have to go at all?' There was a reason Liz didn't approve of fairs – something to do with either goldfish or equal opportunities, though Romula couldn't be bothered to remember which. Romula was going to the fair, and that was that. Everyone was going to the fair.

'Who else is there to go with?' said Romula, snarling.

'Jo,' said Liz. 'Since you insist on being heterosexual.' Jo was Liz's friend Evelyn's boy. He was training to be a social worker. He was sensitive and caring, and stuttered.

'I like Sylvie and I don't like Jo,' said Romula. 'And Jo may be what you see as heterosexual but I don't and nor does Sylvie.'

Honestly, she was a misfit: a prawn in a pool of gleaming trout. What her mother had to put up with!

I do all I can but I'm not what I am!

And then Romula had a really big row with her mother. Liz had just read Romula's school report. Romula had a sweet disposition (*Liz: They must be joking!*), a caring nature, was popular with friends and teachers, and tried hard at lessons. She had an A in Housecraft (now a unisex subject after Liz's letters to the school), a D in Biology, and E's in Chemistry and Physics. (*Liz: They're doing it on purpose. They must be!*)

'Romula,' said Liz, 'you are an embarrassment to me and always have been and that's that!'

'I suppose you wish you'd never had me,' said Romula.

'I wouldn't go as far as that,' said Liz. 'But it might have been easier if you'd been a boy, and I never thought I'd live to hear myself say that. I should have groaned when you came out, not cheered. Go to the fair, if that's what you want, and good riddance.'

Romula gelled her hair and went to the fair in a short mauve frilly skirt and white lace top borrowed from Sylvie. She had to wear her trainers because that was all she had and she was a size 7 and Sylvie a size 3, but they looked okay. She wore a glass diamond ring on each finger: and, such was the magic of her hands, they didn't look cheap and nasty at all.

It was a warm excited night: honky-tonk tunes and sentimental ballads fought it out between and over the rides, the stalls, the shrieks and screams, the arcade machines. The lights on the ground dimmed the moon into nothingness. The site was crowded, but not so you couldn't move. Romula and Sylvie had paper money in their pockets. Romula felt quite peculiar: elated and ashamed by the last thing she'd said to her mother: for some reason it made her skip about.

'I'd have left you too if I'd been my father.'

'He didn't leave, I threw him out.'

'I don't believe you,' cried Romula in triumph. 'You made him feel useless, you made him feel wretched, so he left, and I expect now he's the happiest man in the world. I hope he is!'

That'd teach her! Mother, stony-faced dragon in jeans and a sweatshirt. But she was a good woman too: she worked at the Well Woman Centre, for the love of people (well, women), not money. You had to acknowledge it. Only not just now, just not tonight, the night of the fair.

Sylvie and Romula stopped by the Super Disco Waltzer, and fathers with children on their shoulders brushed by (and Sylvie shrieked because now there was candy floss in her hair). And they wondered if they dared.

I do what I dare and I am what I am.

The floor of the Waltzer rotated, faster and faster round its mirrored central pivot, and from its central mirrored pivot music streamed, and jets of steam which spurted out rainbow fog, and through the fog the murmur of a female voice – 'You want to go faster? Scream louder! Scream louder!' – poured like soft liquid over the clutching, shrieking, dizzy riders, and the louder they screamed the faster they spun, for as the floor rotated it rose and fell: and on this moving, surging base the open cars rotated and spun; and disco lights and spotlights swung and danced and raced from the whirling ceiling above: and all of a sudden Romula saw the ride attendants, the Princes of the Fair, one for every three cars, the young men who rode the Waltzer for their fairground living, who battled with the surging floor like fishermen in a storm, dancing and leaping to stay in the same place; their task to spin the cars as they passed.

'Fixed orbit satellites,' said Romula to Sylvie. (Romula paid attention in Physics whenever the subject left the ground. Above a hundred feet and Romula listened. So our vocations make their

presence known in early life.) As for Sylvie, she had no idea what
Romula was talking about. How could she?

Romula thought she'd never seen anything so beautiful, so magical
as the young men, strong, lithe, muscled, not a brain in their
heads, as Liz would have said, and who cared? She thought she
would faint. The men lunged and pushed, and round and round
them went the cars like crazy things, with the white stunned faces
of the riders appearing and disappearing as they spun.
'You're scared,' said Sylvie. 'Too scared to have a go on the Super
Disco Waltzer!'
'I'm not,' said Romula, but she was, she was – of her future, her
past, of sex, of men, of life, of her mother, of everything. And well
she might be. It's terrifying.

I am what I dare but I'm not what I hope.

'Men love women for their future,' Romula said to me over
breakfast, 'women love men for their past.' Bad news but true, I
thought, though who wants to know it? What enchanted Romula
about the Riders was not just what they were but 'where they'd
been I couldn't go, what they felt I'd never know'; not just the
blue tattoos flashing on their strong arms under the disco lights
as they spun the cars and leapt like fish over waves to keep their
balance – 'really they were like dancers' – or the gleam of white
teeth and red mouth, or the moving of buttocks beneath tight jeans
– all of that yet none of that. Something more.
'I can't explain except to say I loved Ben for his past, and his
strangeness, and his newness, not just his muscles or the tattoos
on his arm, and the ground which was like waves and his mastery
over it.'

'I'm not scared one bit,' said Romula, and they paid their £2 each
(the most expensive ride of the fair, and not surprising) and when
the cars finally slowed, and sighed, and stopped, they got in, and
Romula's little white hands closed softly around the metal bar.
And Ben, top Waltzer Rider, didn't just twist the car but rode the
car, bewitched, mesmerized and enchanted by Romula's white
hands beside his own strong brown ones. After they'd shrieked

their fill he took Romula down by the canal, and Romula would have died if he hadn't.

'Do what you can and be what you are,' said Ben to Romula. 'Life's simpler than you think. Time you left home, anyway.'

'AIDS!' shrieked Liz. 'AIDS!' Why did Romula tell her? God knows. Girls shouldn't talk to their mothers as if they were sisters. They're mothers. As you grow up they grow old. They don't like it. More chances for you, fewer chances for them.

But there wasn't anything Liz could do, and she was going away for a seminar anyway, on 'Yoga – a replacement for tranquillizers?' and Evelyn and her son Jo were moving in to keep an eye on Romula.

I'll do what I want and be what I am.

So every day that week Romula met Ben and she was quite giddy with love and he was quite giddy with something, but the fair was moving on as fairs will: and besides he was married: but somehow the parting seemed right: the grief that followed healing more things than just Romula losing Ben. Round the cars whizzed on the surging floor, faster and faster, big male hands and little white girl fingers.

And every day that week Romula went into the new tattooist who'd opened up in the High Street – 'New needles every customer – free!' – and flourishing the fake passport which was sixth-form common property proved herself over eighteen and had a dragon, like the one on Ben's right buttock, tattooed on the back of her left hand. Amazing how you can keep a left hand out of sight if you try.

But you couldn't hide it from a mother for long and when Liz came home she went mad, and threw Romula out of the house. Only temporarily, of course. Afterwards, in remorse, she took Romula on holiday to Greece, to Lesbos.
'I shouldn't have gone away when I did,' lamented Liz. 'Always looking after other people, neglecting my own child.'

Friends assured her she was wrong, it wasn't like that at all, and they were right, of course. New advances in cosmetic surgery must surely before long make tattoos removable; the dragon wouldn't be there for life.
But it was, it was: the veins in her hand ran straight to her heart: it was there in her heart for ever.

I do what I can and I am what I am.

The journey to Lesbos was Romula's first air flight. Lesbos was tedious, but Romula, gazing at the dragon on her hand, loving Ben, lost for always, for ever and ever, fell in love with flying, and the men who leapt so high above the waves they could stay in the air for ever. 'A conversion experience', was how she described it. The kind of thing, sceptics would say, that sometimes happens when unhappiness is too much to bear. But I don't see it like that. I think she was just born to fly.

Be that as it may, when Romula said she was dropping science and planned to be an air hostess, her mother just said, 'Okay. If that's what you really want. Do what you can and be what you are, and good luck to you.'

The Year of the Green Pudding

The Personnel Department? This way? Thanks.

Sir, you have a nice face. I reckon I can talk to you. Tell you about myself? Why not! That's what you're there for, after all.

It must be possible to live on this earth without doing anyone any damage. It must be. I try to be good. I really try. I rescue wasps from glasses of cider, I look where I'm going so I don't tread on ants. The second worst sound I ever heard was when I went to rescue a lamb tangled up in an electric fence, and there was a crackle, crackle underfoot and I was treading on snails, cracking their shells, piercing them, killing them. Why did so many snails congregate in one spot? There was no reason I could see, except mass suicide. But no excuses for me: I should have looked where I was going: the lamb could have waited a second longer: the snails would have been saved. The second worst thing I ever did was murder a duckling. Not on purpose, of course, but definitely murder by neglect. No excuses. I went to put the ducks away for the night, to save them from the fox. I heard a cheep-cheep and assumed it came from inside the shed. I should have checked. I didn't. The sound came from *under* the shed. I was deaf to the cheep, cheep, cheep, the little plea for help as darkness fell and the bright eyes of predators gathered in the hedge. I wanted to get back into the warm for a cup of coffee. In the morning there was no duckling. I reckon the rat took it, that blonde little, silly little helpless thing. I saw the rat later, a great fat brown hairy mean thing, and I let it go. I could have taken a stick and beaten it to death. But it had a right to live. Why should the rat's ugliness, the duckling's prettiness, condemn the rat to death? Yes, sir, I was brought up in the country.

What was the worst sound I ever heard? It was the sound of Cynthia's crying outside her bedroom door, while I lay inside with her husband. Crocus we called him. He had a thick thatch of yellow hair, which brightened up dull rooms. Cynthia was my best friend, so you understand the 'we'. The worst thing I ever did? Why, to be there with him in the bed.

I'm a middling sort of person, don't you think, sir? Of middle height and middle size, and I buy the kind of clothes that are labelled S, M or L; kind of floppy, not tailored. I choose the M. My hair, left to its own devices, is mid-brown and my shoes are size five, the middle size they say, though I think statistically sixes are more normal now. Our research department says the population's getting bigger. My eyes are a kind of middle grey and I wear a medium make-up base. Really I'm sometimes surprised family and friends recognize me in the street. I smile a lot, as you'll have noticed, showing these middling-even teeth, but my friends sometimes complain I have no sense of humour. I just think they're sometimes not very funny in what they say and do. For instance, I think Irish jokes are dangerous and cruel and I also think one has to say so, out loud, there and then, if anyone begins. There's one joke I heard recently which did make me laugh, out loud. It goes like this. 'Question: How many radical feminists does it take to change a lightbulb? Answer: That's not funny.' So I do have a sense of humour. Anyway, that's enough about me.

Why am I here? My department head sent me to discuss my resignation. Did I mention that I'm a vegetarian? No? Actually I try to be a vegan (that's someone who doesn't eat any dairy foods, never mind just the cow itself, both on health grounds and because if eating the cow is murder, drinking the milk is theft), but I don't always succeed. I'm like A. A. Milne's king – 'I do like a little bit of butter on my bread.' I hope all this doesn't make me sound rigid and boring; I don't honestly believe I am. I just do try to get by doing as little damage as I can. And I make a very good onion and potato pie!

That's since Crocus. Not the pie, the not doing damage. What happened about Crocus was this. I was twenty-five. A funny sort

of age: not really young, but not really old: just too old to enter
the best beauty contests. I felt more on the shelf then than I have
done before or since, I don't know why. Cynthia, as I say, was my
best friend. She and Crocus had a little boy of two, Matthew.
They'd had to get married because Matthew was on the way.
Cynthia wasn't much good with babies, and I was round there a
lot helping. I wasn't married, I had no children, I was just more
competent than she was. It wasn't difficult. She once put salt in
his bottle instead of sugar. She shouldn't have put sugar in anyway:
it's unnecessary and fattens without nourishing, but try and tell
Cynthia anything like that. Cynthia wasn't middling to look
at, not at all. Cynthia was narrow-waisted and long-legged and
long-backed and had natural blonde hair, one of those white,
fragile skins which go with it, and dark blue eyes, the blue you
see when you look out of Concorde's window. (I have been in
Concorde: I am full of surprises. Crocus used to say I was full of
surprises.) I talk of Crocus in the past tense because it's all over
between him and me, and Cynthia's in the past tense because
she's all over. She's dead. What happened was this. I know I'm a
long time getting round to it, I'm sorry, it's just so dreadful, I
rattle on and put it off.

Concorde? I was working on the Liver Pâté Account. They were
serving it on Concorde, on little pieces of toast, with free champagne cocktails. The client offered me a free flight. Why are you
so interested in Concorde?

Cynthia went into hospital to have her second baby. She'd had a
dreadful pregnancy, poor thing; the baby was pressing on the
sciatic nerve. I moved in to look after little Matthew – and Crocus.
Cook meals – you know how men are not supposed to be able to.
Though if you ask me they just don't want it known quite how
good they are, in case it gets around. She was in for forty-eight
hours. I think Crocus and me could have got through that, even
though we were alone. I mean talking formally and not catching
each other's eye, though what he wanted was to be in bed with
me and what I wanted was to be in bed with him, and we both
knew it. Not saying, not touching, made it stronger; that's the way
it goes. The whole air crackled between us. But we could have

held out, I know we could. Cynthia would have come back and it would all just have faded away. Things do. But the hospital rang and said the baby wasn't up to its birth weight: Cynthia wouldn't be back till Saturday. That was the Wednesday. And on Wednesday night, after visiting hour – he'd taken chocolates (Crocus was like Cynthia: he never would believe just how bad sugar is for you) and I'd taken grapes – we came straight back and went to bed together. Not the spare room – it was too near Matthew's room – but their bed, Crocus and Cynthia's bed. I told you about his hair, didn't I? Blonde! Cynthia had dark-red pillowslips. I shall never forget – And Thursday evening we went to see her again, at visiting time, with never a flicker, all that sex didn't seem any of her business somehow, and the new baby was just lovely and Matthew seemed really fond of it – it was a girl – and Cynthia said she wanted to call her after me because I was such a good friend and, do you know, I felt not a twinge of guilt. Does that make me odd, or just like anyone else? I didn't mean to hurt her, but Crocus and me – it just seemed more important than anything else: what made the world go round and the stars shine and the wind blow and so forth. And all of Friday, when Matthew was at playgroup, and as soon as he'd been put down at six o'clock, we were in the bedroom – actually not in the bed most of the time, on the floor – does that make it better or worse? And then suddenly the door opened and there was Cynthia and the baby. She'd discharged herself, we later heard: I don't think because she suspected anything, she just didn't like hospital food – not enough sugar, I suppose – and knew the baby was doing fine in spite of what the hospital said.

She shut the door quickly so she couldn't see us – it took us some time to get ourselves together, or rather not-together – and we could hear her weeping the other side of the door. Just quietly weeping.

Crocus went out to her, but she didn't stay, she just handed him the baby and left. And by the time I'd got myself together – I never was a fast dresser – and he'd handed the baby to me and was gone after her, it was too late. She went down the Underground and threw herself under a train. The poor driver. I think of the poor drivers when anything like that happens.

Anyway, that was that, sir. Crocus couldn't bear to be in the same room with me afterwards, and I think I'd have screamed if he'd touched me. It just sort of shook us right out of it. The young one didn't get called after me, that's all I know. And that she'd been on antidepressants and had threatened suicide in the past. Neither of them had told me that. So what sort of friendship was it? Do you think they were ashamed, or something? Shouldn't you be frank, with friends?

But that was the end of my love life, at least for a time. It put me right off men, I can tell you. I got the blame, of course, and it ought to have been forty per cent of the blame – fifty per cent each and an extra ten per cent for him because he betrayed a marriage partner which is worse than betraying a friend. But of course I got a hundred per cent of it from all and sundry, especially sundry, especially men. I moved out of the district and I got a job here. I'd always wanted to work in an advertising agency. But now I have to resign. Why? I'll tell you.

I do believe if you try, sir, if you really try, you can get through life without causing damage. I just hadn't been trying over the Cynthia/Crocus business. I did, after that, I promise you. I checked up on all my dates; if they said they were married I wouldn't go out with them, I wouldn't even be alone with them. If they said they weren't married, or divorced, I still checked up on them. Thirty per cent who said they weren't, were, can you imagine that? And the other seventy per cent – I just wasn't interested. I was working as a secretary then, sir, not a copywriter as I am now, but hoping, always hoping! Yes, I do get to meet the clients. I suppose I am attractive, in my middling kind of way. You know how it is – there'd be business lunches, business dinners: but I'd just go off home, I was so discouraged, frightened of trouble. I think that client who sent me off on Concorde got really cross, but I couldn't help that. If you don't feel anything, you don't feel anything. And then I met Martin. You know Martin, he's an Art Group Head here. Attractive? Crocus was nothing compared to Martin. You know how it is, you touch and there's this surge of electricity – it's almost as if you've been stung? And I thought to myself, look, I can't go on atoning for ever for what

I did to Cynthia and her children, if I did; because that's what I've been doing. I've got to have children of my own, get married, settled, some time. And Martin was crazy about me. And I was crazy about him. And I thought this is really working, really something – you know that kind of confidence you get when everything's in balance?

And then he told me he was married. I hadn't checked up, I didn't want to check up, I didn't want to know. But he told me. He said theirs was an open marriage, she didn't mind. I minded. I said no, that's it, that's the end. He said go and visit her: and I said no. What would she do if I visited her? Walk straight under the nearest train?
'No,' I said. 'Never.'
He brought her round to me. She said I was welcome to him. She'd met somebody else: she wanted a divorce. I was to feel free, to make her feel better.

So I felt free. By God, I felt free. At last, it seemed to me, a penance which I thought was endless had worked itself out. I was free to be happy. The anxiety lifted. I hadn't realized what it was, this black terrible cloud I'd been living under. Anxiety. If you've suffered from it you'll know what it's like: if you haven't, sir, count your blessings. It's like a physical pain, only it's attached to your feelings, and there's no cure for it, because it has no reality, no real cause in the outside world, so you're free to attach it to any number of things. But what are you anxious *about*? they ask. The answer you give is aircrashes, or AIDS, or you've forgotten to turn the gas off, or you've offended your best friend (that's always a good one for me) but the answer is, it's not *about* anything, it's just anxiety, free-floating anxiety, and you'd rather be dead but you don't try because you're too anxious about failing. I guess Cynthia wasn't anxious. Just depressed. But Martin cured me of every sad, negative feeling I ever had. It's been a wonderful year, a whole year of happiness. We became proper vegans together; we jogged, being careful not to step on snails; we joined the League Against Cruel Sports, until we decided it was cruel to humans; and I taught Martin not to kill wasps but just to sit still and leave them alone and they'll leave you alone, and to pick spiders out of the bath with a postcard and cup. Then you lot gave me promotion at work. I actually became a copywriter! It seemed to me I could love Martin and do nobody any harm.

But now it's January the second and I have to hand in my notice to you, sir. I have to, sir. This is what happened. Haven't you heard? You know I'm on the Fresh Ginger Account, sir? And that we took all those full-page spreads in the women's magazines? And that I did the recipe for the Christmas Pudding? And that it went in in July, so that everyone's puddings would have time to mature by Christmas? I didn't check the recipe, sir. I was too happy with Martin to bother. I remember thinking, shall I check this through once again or shall I quickly, quickly go downstairs to the canteen and meet him for a drink. You get somehow starved of some people, at a certain stage in a relationship, and really suffer if you can't see and touch and be with them. And that was the stage Martin and I were at. And I didn't check the recipe. I forgot to put the sugar in. The typist left that line out and I didn't check. And, sir, those full-page spreads are read by tens of millions, and one in ten actually made the pudding, covered it with foil, left it to mature, put it in boiling water on Christmas morning, turned it out piping-hot after the turkey, and it was green. Green. Mould. Inedible. Green puddings by the million, sir, and my fault. A million family Christmases spoiled, because I was in love.

Yes, I said was. Every bit of feeling's vanished. I don't think I could bear to touch Martin now. I don't know what it was all about, all that feeling, all that kissing, all that love. Except I seem doomed to cause trouble. I'm never going to fall in love again, sir, never, never, never.

Sir, there is a little brown spider by your elbow. Don't move, you might squash it.

FOUR TALES FROM ABROAD

Ind Aff
or Out of Love in Sarajevo

This is a sad story. It has to be. It rained in Sarajevo, and we had expected fine weather.

The rain filled up Sarajevo's pride, two footprints set into a pavement, marking the spot where the young assassin Princip stood to shoot the Archduke Ferdinand and his wife. (Don't forget his wife: everyone forgets his wife, the Archduchess.) That happened in the summer of 1914. Sarajevo is a pretty town, Balkan style, mountain-rimmed. A broad, swift, shallow river runs through its centre, carrying the mountain snows away. The river is arched by many bridges and the one nearest the two footprints has been named The Princip Bridge. The young man is a hero in these parts. Not only does he bring in the tourists – look, look, the spot, the very spot! – but by his action, as everyone knows, he lit the spark which fired the timber which caused World War I which crumbled the Austro-Hungarian Empire, the crumbling of which made modern Yugoslavia possible. Forty million dead (or was it thirty?), but who cares? So long as he loved his country.

The river, they say, can run so shallow in the summer it's known derisively as 'the wet road'. Today, from what I could see through the sheets of falling rain, it seemed full enough. Yugoslavian streets are always busy – no one stays home if they can help it (thus can an indecent shortage of housing space create a sociable nation) and it seemed that as if by common consent a shield of bobbing umbrellas had been erected two metres high to keep the rain off the streets. But the shield hadn't worked around Princip's corner, that was plain.

'Come all this way,' said Peter, who was a Professor of Classical History, 'and you can't even see the footprints properly, just two undistinguished puddles.' Ah, but I loved him. I shivered for his disappointment. He was supervising my thesis on varying concepts of morality and duty in the early Greek states as evidenced in their poetry and drama. I was dependent upon him for my academic future. Peter said I had a good mind but not a first-class mind, and somehow I didn't take it as an insult. I had a feeling first-class minds weren't all that good in bed.

Sarajevo is in Bosnia, in the centre of Yugoslavia, that grouping of unlikely states, that distillation of languages into the phonetic reasonableness of Serbo-Croat. We'd sheltered from the rain in an ancient mosque in Serbian Belgrade: done the same in a monastery in Croatia: now we spent a wet couple of days in Sarajevo beneath other people's umbrellas. We planned to go on to Montenegro, on the coast, where the fish and the artists come from, to swim and lie in the sun, and recover from the exhaustion caused by the sexual and moral torments of the last year. It couldn't possibly go on raining for ever. Could it? Satellite pictures showed black cloud swishing gently all over Europe, over the Balkans, into Asia – practically all the way from Moscow to London, in fact. It wasn't that Peter and I were being singled out. No. It was raining on his wife, too, back in Cambridge.

Peter was trying to make the decision, as he had been for the past year, between his wife and myself as his permanent life partner. To this end we had gone away, off the beaten track, for a holiday: if not with his wife's blessing, at least with her knowledge. Were we really, truly suited? We had to be sure, you see, that this was more than just any old professor-student romance: that it was the Real Thing, because the longer the indecision went on the longer Mrs Piper, Peter said, would be left dangling in uncertainty and distress. He and she had been married for twenty-four years; they'd stopped loving each other a long time ago, naturally – but there would be a fearful personal and practical upheaval entailed if he decided to leave permanently and shack up, as he put it, with me. Which I wanted him to do, because I loved him. And so far I was winning hands down. It didn't seem much of a contest at all, in fact. I'd been cool and thin and informed on the seat next to him in a Zagreb theatre (Mrs Piper was sweaty and only liked TV), was now eager and anxious for social and political instruction in Sarajevo (Mrs Piper spat in the face of knowledge, Peter had once told me), and planned to be lissom and topless – I hadn't quite decided: it might be counterproductive to underline the age differential – while I splashed and shrieked like a bathing belle in the shallows of the craggy Croatian coast (Mrs Piper was a swimming coach: I imagined she smelt permanently of chlorine).

So far as I could see it was no contest at all between his wife and myself. How could he possibly choose her while I was on offer? But Peter liked to luxuriate in guilt and indecision. And I loved him with an inordinate affection, and indulged him in this luxury.

Princip's footprints are a metre apart, placed like the feet of a modern cop on a training shoot-out – the left in front at a slight outward angle, the right behind, facing forward. There seemed great energy focused here. Both hands on the gun, run, stop, plant the feet, aim, fire! I could see the footprints well enough, in spite of Peter's complaint. They were clear enough to me, albeit puddled.

We went to a restaurant for lunch, since it was too wet to do what we loved to do: that is, buy bread, cheese, sausage, wine and go off somewhere in our hired car, into the woods or the hills, and picnic and make love. It was a private restaurant – Yugoslavia went over to a mixed capitalist–communist economy years back, so you get either the best or the worst of both systems, depending on your mood – that is to say, we knew we would pay more but be given a choice. We chose the wild boar.

'Probably ordinary pork soaked in red cabbage water to darken it,' said Peter. He was not in a good mood.
Cucumber salad was served first.
'Everything in this country comes with cucumber salad,' complained Peter. I noticed I had become used to his complaining. I supposed that when you had been married a while you simply wouldn't hear it. He was forty-six and I was twenty-five.

'They grow a lot of cucumber,' I said.

'If they can grow cucumbers,' Peter then asked, 'why can't they grow mange-tout?' It seemed a why-can't-they-eat-cake sort of argument to me, but not knowing enough about horticulture not to be outflanked if I debated the point, I moved the subject on to safer ground.

'I suppose Princip's action couldn't really have started World War One,' I remarked. 'Otherwise, what a thing to have on your conscience! One little shot and the deaths of thirty million on your shoulders.'

'Forty,' he corrected me. Though how they reckon these things and get them right I can't imagine. 'Of course Princip didn't start the war. That's just a simple tale to keep the children quiet. It takes more than an assassination to start a war. What happened was that the build-up of political and economic tensions in the Balkans was such that it had to find some release.'

'So it was merely the shot that lit the spark that fired the timber that started the war, et cetera?'

'Quite,' he said. 'World War One would have had to have started sooner or later.'

'A bit later or a bit sooner', I said, 'might have made the difference of a million or so: if it was you on the battlefield in the mud and the rain you'd notice: exactly when they fired the starting-pistol: exactly when they blew the final whistle. Is that what they do when a war ends: blow a whistle? So that everyone just comes in from the trenches?'

But he wasn't listening. He was parting the flesh of the soft collapsed orangey-red pepper which sat in the middle of his cucumber salad; he was carefully extracting the pips. He didn't like eating pepper pips. His Nan had once told him they could never be digested, would stick to the wall of his stomach and do terrible damage. I loved him for his vulnerability, the bit of him that was forever little boy: I loved him for his dexterity and patience with his knife and fork. I'd finished my salad yonks ago, pips and all. I was hungry. I wanted my wild boar.

Peter might have been forty-six but he was six foot two and well-muscled and grizzled with it, in a dark-eyed, intelligent, broad-jawed kind of way. I adored him. I loved to be seen with him. 'Muscular-academic, not weedy-academic,' as my younger sister Clare once said. 'Muscular-academic is just a generally superior human being: everything works well from the brain to the toes. Weedy-academic is when there isn't enough vital energy in the person, and the brain drains all the strength from the other parts.' Well, Clare should know. Clare is only twenty-three, but of the superior human kind herself, vividly pretty, bright and competent – somewhere behind a heavy curtain of vibrant, as they say, red hair, which she only parts for effect. She had her first degree at twenty. Now she's married to a Harvard Professor of Economics seconded to the United Nations. She can even cook. I gave up competing when she was fourteen and I was sixteen. Though she too is capable of self-deception. I would say her husband was definitely of the weedy-academic rather than the muscular-academic type. And they have to live in Brussels.

The Archduke's chauffeur had lost his way, and was parked on the corner trying to recover his nerve when Princip came running out of a café, planted his feet, aimed and fired. Princip was seventeen – too young to hang. But they sent him to prison for life and, since he had TB to begin with, he only lasted three years. He died in 1917, in a Swiss prison. Or perhaps it was more than TB: perhaps they gave him a hard time, not learning till later, when the Austro-Hungarian Empire collapsed, that he was a hero. Poor Princip, too young to die – like so many other millions. Dying for love of a country.

'I love you,' I said to Peter, my living man, progenitor already of three children by his chlorinated, swimming-coach wife.
'How much do you love me?'
'Inordinately! I love you with inordinate affection.'
It was a joke between us. Ind Aff!
'Inordinate affection is a sin,' he'd told me. 'According to the Wesleyans. John Wesley himself worried about it to such a degree that he ended up abbreviating it in his diaries. Ind Aff. He maintained that what he felt for young Sophy, the eighteen-year-old in his congregation, was not Ind Aff, which bears the spirit

away from God towards the flesh: no, what he felt was a pure and spiritual, if passionate, concern for Sophy's soul.'

Peter said now, as we waited for our wild boar, and he picked over his pepper, 'Your Ind Aff is my wife's sorrow, that's the trouble.' He wanted, I knew, one of the long half wrangles, half soul-sharings that we could keep going for hours, and led to piercing pains in the heart which could only be made better in bed. But our bedroom at the Hotel Europa was small and dark and looked out into the well of the building – a punishment room if ever there was one. (Reception staff did sometimes take against us.) When Peter had tried to change it in his quasi-Serbo-Croat, they'd shrugged their Bosnian shoulders and pretended not to understand, so we'd decided to put up with it. I did not fancy pushing hard single beds together – it seemed easier not to have the pain in the heart in the first place.

'Look,' I said, 'this holiday is supposed to be just the two of us, not Mrs Piper as well. Shall we talk about something else?'

Do not think that the Archduke's chauffeur was merely careless, an inefficient chauffeur, when he took the wrong turning. He was, I imagine, in a state of shock, fright and confusion. There had been two previous attempts on the Archduke's life since the cavalcade had entered town. The first was a bomb which got the car in front and killed its driver. The second was a shot, fired by none other than young Princip, which had missed. Princip had vanished into the crowd and gone to sit down in a corner café, where he ordered coffee to calm his nerves. I expect his hand trembled at the best of times – he did have TB. (Not the best choice of assassin, but no doubt those who arrange these things have to make do with what they can get.) The Archduke's chauffeur panicked, took the wrong road, realized what he'd done, and stopped to await rescue and instructions just, as it happened, outside the café where Princip sat drinking his coffee.

'What shall we talk about?' asked Peter, in even less of a good mood.
'The collapse of the Austro-Hungarian Empire?' I suggested. 'How does an Empire collapse? Is there no money to pay the military

or the police, so everyone goes home? Or what?' He liked to be asked questions.

'The Hungro-Austrian Empire,' said Peter to me, 'didn't so much collapse as fail to exist any more. War destroys social organizations. The same thing happened after World War Two. There being no organizing bodies left between Moscow and London – and for London read Washington, then as now – it was left to these two to put in their own puppet governments. Yalta, 1944. It's taken the best part of forty-five years for nations of Western and Eastern Europe to remember who they are.'

'Austro-Hungarian,' I said, 'not Hungro-Austrian.'

'I didn't say Hungro-Austrian,' he said.

'You did,' I said.

'Didn't,' he said. 'What the hell are they doing about our wild boar? Are they out in the hills shooting it?'

My sister Clare had been surprisingly understanding about Peter. When I worried about him being older, she pooh-poohed it; when I worried about him being married, she said, 'Just go for it, sister. If you can unhinge a marriage, it's ripe for unhinging; it would happen sooner or later; it might as well be you. See a catch, go ahead and catch! Go for it!'

Princip saw the Archduke's car parked outside, and went for it. Second chances are rare in life: they must be responded to. Except perhaps his second chance was missing in the first place? He could have taken his cue from fate, and just sat and finished his coffee, and gone home to his mother. But what's a man to do when he loves his country? Fate delivered the Archduke into his hands: how could he resist it? A parked car, a uniformed and medalled chest, the persecutor of his country – how could Princip, believing God to be on his side, not see this as His intervention, push his coffee aside and leap to his feet?

Two waiters stood idly by and watched us waiting for our wild boar. One was young and handsome in a mountainous Bosnian way – flashing eyes, hooked nose, luxuriant black hair, sensuous mouth. He was about my age. He smiled. His teeth were even and white. I smiled back and, instead of the pain in the heart I'd become accustomed to as an erotic sensation, now felt, quite violently, an associated yet different pang which got my lower stomach. The true, the real pain of Ind Aff!

'Fancy him?' asked Peter.

'No,' I said. 'I just thought if I smiled the wild boar might come quicker.'

The other waiter was older and gentler: his eyes were soft and kind. I thought he looked at me reproachfully. I could see why. In a world which for once, after centuries of savagery, was finally full of young men, unslaughtered, what was I doing with this man with thinning hair?

'What are you thinking of?' Professor Piper asked me. He liked to be in my head.

'How much I love you,' I said automatically, and was finally aware how much I lied. 'And about the Archduke's assassination,' I went on, to cover the kind of tremble in my head as I came to my senses, 'and let's not forget his wife, she died too – how can you say World War One would have happened anyway? If Princip hadn't shot the Archduke something else, some undisclosed, unsuspected variable, might have come along and defused the whole political/military situation, and neither World War One nor Two would ever have happened. We'll just never know, will we?'

I had my passport and my traveller's cheques with me. (Peter felt it was less confusing if we each paid our own way.) I stood up, and took my raincoat from the peg.

'Where are you going?' he asked, startled.

'Home,' I said. I kissed the top of his head, where it was balding. It smelt gently of chlorine, which may have come from thinking about his wife so much, but might merely have been because he'd taken a shower that morning. ('The water all over Yugoslavia, though safe to drink, is unusually highly chlorinated': guide book.) As I left to catch a taxi to the airport the younger of the two waiters emerged from the kitchen with two piled plates of roasted wild boar, potatoes duchesse, and stewed peppers. ('Yugoslavian diet is unusually rich in proteins and fats': guide book.) I could tell from the glisten of oil that the food was no longer hot, and I was not tempted to stay, hungry though I was. Thus fate – or was it Bosnian wilfulness? – confirmed the wisdom of my intent.

And that was how I fell out of love with my professor, in Sarajevo, a city to which I am grateful to this day, though I never got to see much of it, because of the rain.

It was a silly sad thing to do, in the first place, to confuse mere passing academic ambition with love: to try and outdo my sister Clare. (Professor Piper was spiteful, as it happened, and did his best to have my thesis refused, but I went to appeal, which he never thought I'd dare to do, and won. I had a first-class mind after all.) A silly sad episode, which I regret. As silly and sad as Princip, poor young man, with his feverish mind, his bright tubercular cheeks, and his inordinate affection for his country, pushing aside his cup of coffee, leaping to his feet, taking his gun in both hands, planting his feet, aiming and firing – one, two, three shots and starting World War I. The first one missed, the second got the wife (never forget the wife), and the third got the Archduke and a whole generation, and their children, and their children's children, and on and on for ever. If he'd just hung on a bit, there in Sarajevo that August day, he might have come to his senses. People do, sometimes quite quickly.

A Visit from Johannesburg
or Mr Shaving's Wives

Marion flew in from Johannesburg to see her two daughters Elspeth and Erin. Marion was sixty-four but you'd never have known it. Her arms were bare, lean and tanned and braceleted with thick bands of gold. She wore silk dresses from Hong Kong and her blue eyes were large and bright with added oestrogen, and she had a brand-new husband who owned a gold mine. She said she just had to get out of South Africa for a time: Mandela was free and all hell about to break out: this always happened when there was a weak government.

Marion looked at the way her daughters lived and was shocked. Neither was married. They lived together in a country cottage: Elspeth bred sheepdogs and Erin worked in the local school library. Neither looked after her appearance. Elspeth was thirty-eight and had hairy legs and her clothes smelled of damp dog, and Erin was thirty-five and at least two stone overweight. In the evenings they ate beans on toast and watched television.
'You girls ought to be married,' said Marion, aghast.
'There's no one around here to want to marry us,' said Elspeth and Erin, 'and, if there were, we might not want to marry them.' Marion had run off from their father Ted when Elspeth was eight and Erin was five, leaving Ted to bring them up. 'What do women need with men or men with women?' he'd asked, all through their childhood.

'They never had a mother's care at the age they needed it most,' said Marion, weeping on the phone to Cas, her new husband. 'I let those girls down. It's all my fault.'
'It's never too late to make amends,' said Cas, who had a cheerful and optimistic disposition.

He comforted his wife as best he could. But Marion was still upset. She called Ted and said how dare he let her daughters get into such a state. Ted said the girls were perfectly happy and Marion was to leave them alone. What she'd begun would just have to take its course.

Marion put off her return flight and said to her girls, 'Life is better with a man. You don't have to earn your own living and there's always sex when you want it and someone to talk to when the day is done.'

They said, 'We like our independence and we talk to each other when the day is done, though we see what you mean about sex. But all the best men are married, and if they're not there's something wrong with them. They're either maniacs or impotent or gay. Or all three.'

'Oh, pshaw!' said Marion, 'there's always someone perfectly decent about,' and in spite of their protests she put them in touch with a dating agency and filled in the forms on their behalf and then had to fly back to Johannesburg, where Cas had been having trouble with the servants. If people are free to work where they will, how do you get them to work for you at all? Marion blamed Mr de Klerk, for letting Mandela out.

'Our mother is a fascist and a reactionary,' said Elspeth, washing and re-washing her best navy jersey to get the dog smell out.

'She seems very lively,' said Erin, picking her way through a mixed green salad without dressing. She was on a diet.

'The wicked often are,' said Elspeth. Elspeth was the one who'd suffered most when their mother left their father, being the elder.

The phone rang and it was the man from Datawhile. A Mr Leonard Shaving had been in touch. He would be pleased to meet both Erin and Elspeth. He would take them both out to lunch at the Crown and Cheese on Sunday. Mr Shaving's height was six foot two, his weight thirteen stone two, his complexion ruddy, his income large, his property various, his visage attractive, and he had a degree in philology.

'That's the plus,' said Elspeth. 'What's the minus?' People had been trying for years to sell her dogs she didn't want.

The man from Datawhile was hesitant. Then he said, 'He has a birthmark on his forehead and has been married three times already.'

Elspeth and Erin thought a little. But they were no longer content with just each other and a life of no change and little excitement: such was the effect of their mother's sudden eruption out of the land of peaches, gold and injustice.

Elspeth said, 'Most men just hit and run: at least this one stays round to marry.'

Erin said, 'I like the sound of a man who doesn't give up.'

Elspeth said, 'In any case, I rather fancy a short-term marriage,' and Erin said, 'Better a divorcee than left on the shelf.'

Both said, 'Mr Gorbachev has a birthmark on his forehead and it's perfectly charming: the whole world agrees.'

Three marriages, they decided, were nothing. Their mother was on her fifth. And what harm could there possibly be in Sunday lunch at the Crown and Cheese?

Mr Shaving was as handsome, rich, charming, tall and intelligent as his description, and his birthmark no more disfiguring than Mr Gorbachev's, but the attraction was between Erin and him, not Elspeth and him, and it was Erin, the librarian, he asked to marry him. Elspeth hid her disappointment from her sister and the very week of the engagement won Best Dog at Crufts for a sheepdog, Fluffy Danube, and was asked out to celebrate by the owner of Runner-Up Best Dog, the terrier Ratty IV, whose old blue jersey was even smellier than hers had been before its thorough washing. The smell of wet dog is comforting.

Marion and Cas flew over for the wedding. Ted wouldn't attend as he didn't want to set eyes on Marion and besides, went nowhere where he was expected to wear a shirt. He had checked up on Mr Shaving and discovered that his three previous wives had hanged themselves. Elspeth and Erin were offended and said that was (a) hearsay, (b) scandal; c) obviously neurotic women would make a beeline for a man as pleasant and kind as Mr Shaving and (d) they were glad Ted wasn't coming to the wedding. Marion pointed out that in Ted's eyes no good could ever come out of anything so speedy and sexy as a Dating Agency: he was an old-fashioned, jealous old fart and leaving him was the best thing she'd ever done.

The wedding day came and Erin was down to a size 12 and the sun shone and everyone rejoiced, and forgot about Ted, and the owner of Ratty IV came along with Elspeth, and there were obviously more wedding bells in the air: but Elspeth did not cancel her subscription to Datawhile: you could never tell. Mr Shaving whisked Erin back to his large country house, where maids did all the work. He did not want his wife to spoil her nails checking out books in the library so Erin gave up her job and spent her time polishing her nails instead, and thinking about Mr Shaving, as he liked her to do. And life was indeed, as her mother had told her, better with a man. She didn't have to spend her time working, and there was usually sex when she wanted it, though not always. In the evenings he was often melancholy so she would keep her thoughts to herself.
'But it's so wonderful when he smiles,' said Erin to Elspeth; 'It's well worth the times when he doesn't.' But Elspeth thought Erin seemed a little, somehow, abstracted, as if more things were Erin's fault than Erin had ever realized.

'He's the kind of man who buttons up his feelings,' Erin wrote to her mother. 'If only sometimes he'd cry and let them go! But you know what men are! They never talk about their emotions.'
'Darling,' Marion wrote back, 'Men hardly ever have feelings: that's why they so seldom let them go. It's not that they want to cry and don't: it's that they just don't want to cry. Sounds to me as if he's turning out to be like Ted – a real depressive!' She and Cas thought they might be getting a divorce. He wanted her to give a party and ask the de Klerks as guests of honour. Marion said she had no intention of honouring the betrayers of white South Africa.

'Take no notice of Marion,' said Elspeth to Erin. 'She's old-fashioned and bitter, and has quarrelled with Cas. Get your husband to talk about himself. Find out why his other marriages failed. Communication, that's what's needed in a marriage. Laugh

together, love together, cry together.' She and Ratty IV's owner
were going to Preparing-for-Marriage classes, organized by the
Church, though they hadn't yet quite decided to marry.
But Mr Shaving wouldn't talk about himself, or his previous wives.
He said life was here and now; and they were married and that
was that. He didn't say he loved her, because, Erin said to Elspeth,
that wasn't his style. Erin told Mr Shaving that she loved him at
least once a day, and she thought it pleased him, though it
embarrassed him.

One day Mr Shaving had to go away on business, or so he said,
but Erin called the man at Datawhile and discovered that Mr
Shaving had kept his file at the Agency open and that he'd made
four contacts since their wedding. How Erin wept and wailed. She
called Marion who said briskly she shouldn't make such a fuss;
this was what marriage was like: had she ever said any different?
Erin called Elspeth, who said contacts didn't necessarily mean
sex: perhaps he took a philological view of marriage. Erin said he
never spoke to her about philology, she didn't know what it was,
how could she find out now she wasn't allowed in the library; she
was on her own in the world, she always had been; how she suffered!
Nobody understood! She called her father but Ted replied, 'You've
made your bed, now lie on it.' It was a bad day for everyone. Some
days are like that.

Mr Shaving came home and seemed astonished at Erin's grief. 'I
married you because you were calm, plump and in control,' he
said. 'Now you are hysterical, thin and full of demands. What has
happened to you?'
'Marriage to you', she replied, 'has happened to me, as it happened
to your other wives. Where are they now?' And she stamped her
foot.
'Dead and gone,' he said, 'since you force my hand. And all died
for love of themselves, not me. Samantha took her life because I
spent a night with Sally Anne; so I married Sally Anne, what else
could I do; but within the year Sally Anne had recourse to the
rope because of her guilt about Samantha, and Sally Anne returned
to haunt my next wife Jennifer, with whom I was when Sally Anne
died, so she lost her wits and swung, and none of them cared for

me enough to contain their own lechery, guilt and folly. They only cared about themselves, and each other.'

'And what are your feelings about your poor dead wives?' asked Erin.

'I have none,' he said. 'They did what they did. We must all take responsibility for our own lives and, as with our lives, our deaths.'

'Try and *feel*,' said Erin, who had been attending a therapy group for the wives of depressives, to Mr Shaving, and she led him to the barn where his wives had one by one swung and dangled from the same stout hook. It was a haunted, gloomy place and oppressed her spirits terribly, and his as well, though he would not admit it.

'I feel nothing,' he said. 'I only behaved as a man behaves when he follows his nose and gets on with his work.'

'Follows his nose nothing,' she said. 'It's something else he follows!'

'Why should a man not?' asked Mr Shaving, 'since it's in his nature so to do? Why can't you be happy with me as I am with you; I fill your pocket and I fill your bed: we even watch telly together. My unconscious is my own, not yours.'

'I married all of you,' she said, 'including that. Including your soul.'

'Oh no, you did not,' he said, and stalked off, as she later heard from Datawhile, to an evening out with an heiress in a seaside town, and he never came back. Divorce papers came with the post. Erin wept and wailed.

'If only I hadn't said this,' she wrote to Marion, 'if only I hadn't done that, he'd still be with me now. If only I'd left his soul alone!'

'His mother hurt him when he came out,' wrote Marion. 'You could tell by the mark on his forehead. It wouldn't matter what you said or what you did, he was born to make women unhappy. Not all men are like that, of course.'

She was happy with Cas again. She'd given the party, and the de Klerks had come and charmed her. Elspeth wrote to Cas and wrote to Ted: 'I'm terribly worried about Erin. She sits in the barn all day feeling sisterly to the three poor dead Mrs Shavings. Supposing she comes out in sympathy, and leaps from the rafters herself?'

Cas and Marion caught a plane straight over from Johannesburg and Ted took his bicycle out of the shed and rode the hundred miles south and they all arrived at the same time, just as Erin was in the barn putting the noose around her neck.

'More men in the sea than ever came out of it,' said Marion, removing the rope. 'If at first you don't succeed, try, try, try again. Anything, that is, but suicide.'

'You were just fine until you married,' said Ted. 'I blame your mother.' But at least he and Marion shook hands and shared a bar of chocolate, and Cas was jovial.

'I'll get you a divorce lawyer, Erin,' said Cas. 'You'll do well out of this!' and Erin quite brightened. It's hard to give up lobster and champagne if you've wasted years on tuna and goats' milk, and you know it: and a relief to realize that income need not stop when marriage does, if that marriage has been to a monster.

Elspeth called Datawhile and got Erin's file reopened at no extra cost. Within a year Erin had remarried; now she was wife to a wealthy left-wing County Councillor with a social conscience; he was a reconstructed man, in the feminist sense. In fact he talked about his responses and his feelings so much, and about how he could best make amends for the sins of his gender, that she sometimes fell asleep before he got round to sex. But, as Marion said, it was probably better this way than the other.

'The greatest thing you'll ever know,' said Marion, 'the hardest thing you'll ever learn, is how to love and be loved in return. Look at me! Five marriages and I made it! I'm so happy I could almost change my politics!'

Au Pair

'It's all a matter of landscape,' Bente's mother Greta wrote to her daughter from her apartment in the outer suburbs of Copenhagen, there where the land tilts gently and gracefully towards a flat northern sea, and the birch trees in spring are an almost unbearably brilliant green, and at night the lights of Sweden glitter across the water, with their promise of sombre wooded crags, and dark ravines, and steeper, more difficult shores altogether. 'The English are dirty because they are so comparatively unobserved. They can hide behind hills from their neighbours. Dirt is normal, Bente, all over the world. It's we in the clean flat lands who are out of step.'

Bente's mother was fanciful. It was one of her many charms. Men loved her absurdities. Her folly made them feel strong and sane. Greta had wide grey eyes and flaxen hair, a good strong figure and a frivolous nature. Her daughter had inherited her mother's looks, but not her nature. Bente's father had been Swedish-born. He had passed on to his daughter, Greta feared, his deep Swedish solemnity, his high Swedish standards. He had been killed in the war. After that, neighbours said then, and still said, Greta had slept with enough German soldiers to man a landing raft: she was lucky to be accepted back into the community. Greta said she had only done these things on the instructions of the Resistance, the better to gain the enemy's secrets. Be that as it may, there was no arguing but that Greta had gained a taste for sex, somewhere along the line; and Bente had not, even by the age of twenty-three, not even with her mother's example to guide her. Bente was glad to get away from Copenhagen and the tread of male footsteps on her mother's stair, and to come as an au pair to London, the better to learn the language. And Greta was glad enough to see her stunning, unsmiling daughter go.

But within a week Bente rang in tears to say that the Beavers' household was dirty, the food was uneatable, she was expected to sleep in a damp dark basement room, she was overworked and underpaid, and the two children were unruly, unkempt, and objected to taking baths.
'Then clean the house,' said Greta firmly. 'Take over the cooking and the accounts, move a mattress to a better room, and bath the children by force if necessary, or better still get in the bath with them. The English are too afraid of nakedness.'

Bente sobbed on the other end of the line, and Greta's sailor lover, Mogens, moved an impatient hand up her thigh. Greta had told Mogens she'd had Bente when she was seventeen. 'But I want to come home,' said Bente, and Greta said sharply that surely Bente could put up with a little dirt and discomfort. Adrian Beaver was a Marxist sociologist/journalist with an international reputation and Bente should think herself lucky to be in so interesting a household and not abuse her employers' hospitality by making too many long distance calls on their telephone. Greta put down the phone and turned her attention to Mogens. Lovers come and go: children go on for ever!

There was silence for a month or so, during which time Greta, feeling just a little guilty, sent Bente a leather mini-skirt and a recipe for steak au poivre using green pepper, and a letter explaining her theories on dirt and landscape.

Bente's next letter home was cheerful enough: she asked Greta to send her some root ginger, since this was unobtainable in the outer London suburbs where she lived and she had only four hours off a week, and that on Sundays, and could not easily get into central London where most exotic ingredients were available. Mr Beaver was developing quite a taste for good food. Mrs Beaver had objected to her wearing the mini-skirt, so Bente only wore it in her absence. Mr Beaver worked at home: life was much easier now that Mrs Beaver had a full-time job. She, Bente, could take over.

The house was spick and span. When she, Bente, had children, she, Bente, would never leave them in a stranger's care. But she, Bente, liked to think the children were fond of her. She got into the bath with them, these days, and there was no trouble at all at bath time. Mr Beaver, Adrian, said she was a better mother to the boys than his wife was. She was certainly a better cook!

Greta's new lover, Clifton, from the Caribbean, posted off the ginger without a covering letter. Silence seemed, at the time, golden. Greta knew Bente would just hate Clifton, who was probably not yet twenty, and wonderfully black and shiny. Greta told him she'd had Bente when she was sixteen.

Bente rang in tears to say Mr Beaver kept touching her breasts in the kitchen and embarrassing her and she thought he wanted to sleep with her and could she come home at once?

Greta said what nonsense, sex is a free and wonderful thing: just sleep with him and get it over. There was silence the other end of the line. Clifton's hot breath stirred the hairs on Greta's neck. She knew the flax was beginning to streak with grey. How short life is!
'But what about his wife?' asked Bente, doubtfully, presently.
'Knowing the English as I do,' said Greta, 'they've probably worked it out between them just to stop you handing in your notice.'
'So you don't think she'd mind?'
Clifton's sharp white teeth nibbled Greta's ear and his arm lay black and thick across her silky white breasts.
'Of course not,' said Greta. 'What are you getting so worked up about? Sex is just fun. It's not to be taken seriously.'
'I'm not so sure,' said Bente, primly.
'Bente,' said Greta, 'pillow talk is the best way to learn a foreign language, and that's what you're in England for. Do just be practical, even if you don't know how to enjoy yourself.'
Clifton's teeth dug sharply into Greta's earlobe and she uttered the husky little scream which so entranced and interested men. After she had replaced the receiver, it occurred to Greta that her daughter was still a virgin, and she almost picked up the phone

for a longer talk, but then the time was past and Clifton's red, red tongue was importuning her and she forgot all about Bente for at least a week. Out of sight, out of mind! Many mothers feel it: few acknowledge it!

Bente wrote within the month to ask if she should tell Mrs Beaver that she and Mr Beaver were having an affair, since she didn't like to be deceitful. Adrian himself was reluctant to do it, saying it might upset the children and it should be kept secret. What did Greta think?

Greta wrote back to say, with feeling, that children should not begrudge their parents a sex life; you had to take sex calmly and openly, not get hysterical. Sex is like a wasp, wrote Greta. You must just sit still and let it take its course. It's when you try and brush it away the trouble comes. Fanciful Greta!

Bente wrote to say that Mrs Beaver had moved out of the house: simply abandoned the children and left! What sort of mother was that? She, Bente, would never do such a thing. Mrs Beaver was hopelessly neurotic. (Didn't Greta think her, Bente's, English had improved? She had been quite right about pillow talk!) Mr Beaver had told his wife she could continue living in the spare room and have her own lovers quite freely, but Mrs Beaver hadn't been at all grateful and had made the most dreadful scenes before finally going and had even tried to knife her, Bente, and Mr Beaver had lost half a stone in weight. Could Greta send her the pickled-herring recipe? She enclosed a photograph of herself and Adrian and the boys. She and Adrian were to be married as soon as he was free. Wasn't love wonderful? Wasn't fate an extraordinary thing? Supposing she and Adrian had never met? Supposing this, supposing that!

Greta studied the photograph with a magnifying glass. Adrian Beaver, she was surprised to see, was at least fifty and running to fat, and plain in a peculiarly English, intellectual, chinless way, and the Beaver sons were not little, as she had supposed, but in their early adolescence and ungainly too. Her daughter stood next to Mr Beaver, twice his size, big-busted, bovine, with the sweet inexorable smile of a flaxen doll. Greta did not want to have grandchildren, especially not these grandchildren. Greta, one way and another, was in a fix.

Greta had fallen in love, in a peculiarly high, pure, almost sexless way – who'd have thought it! But life goes this way, now that! – with a doctor from Odense, who wanted to marry her, Greta, save her from herself and build her a house in glass and steel where she could live happily ever after. (Perhaps she was in love with the house, not him, but what could it matter? Love is love, even if it's for glass and steel!) The doctor was thirty-five. Greta, alas, on first meeting him, had given her age as thirty-four. Unless she had given birth to Bente when she was ten, how now could Bente be her daughter?
'You are no daughter of mine,' she wrote back to Bente. 'Sex is one thing, love quite another. Sex may be a wasp, but love is a swarm of bees! You have broken up a marriage, done a dreadful thing! I never wish to hear from you again.'

And nor did she, and both lived happily ever after: the mother in the flat, clean, cheerful land: the daughter in the dirty, hilly, troubled one across the sea, where fate had taken her. How full the world is of bees and wasps! In the autumn the birch trees of Denmark turn russet red and glorious, and the lights which shine across from Sweden seem hard and resolute and the air chilly, and the wasps and bees move slowly and sleepily amongst the red, red leaves, and how lucky you are if you escape a sting!

How I Am is How You Are

'Hello. How are you today?' came from the waiter's mouth. And he didn't quite speak, and he didn't quite murmur, and he didn't quite whine; what he did was *greet*, and he greeted with such a sweet smile, such a generous crumpling of mouth muscles, a squeezing of big brown eyes, you might almost have thought he meant it. But since the guest with the leather hat and the sandals, and the thick hands so battered by the over-use and accidents of decades as to be all but impossible to clean, and the woman in the blue-and-white spotted dress, cartwheel hat and blue-and-white striped shoes, just stared at him, as if taken aback by the question, the waiter flicked his napkin around their empty, perfectly clean table and went away.

'The word "greet" in Scotland means to weep, to grieve, to mourn,' said Aileen.

'I don't follow your train of thought,' he said.

'Well no,' she said, 'I don't suppose you do. Rowena says she likes Mexicans, they're such sweet guys, she personally has nothing against chicanos. Though of course nowadays few people use that term, she says. There are so many immigrants here you never know where any of them come from: seeping up over the border from anywhere in the South, and they all just get lumped together as "Latinos". If you're an illegal you get to be called a silent immigrant, which I suppose is quite polite. Rowena Gersh says there are now thirty million people in Los Angeles County and eighty per cent of them speak Spanish, so the twenty per cent are probably wise to be polite.'

'Which one is Rowena Gersh?'

'Rowena Gersh is my agent.'

'The one with the tiny feet?'

59

'Yes. I expect so. Though I have never noticed her feet. She was here earlier, wishing you good luck.'

'The one who's not coming to my show? She is a bitch. I don't know why you have anything to do with these dreadful people.'

'She's coming later. She's having drinks with Spielberg. Some deal or other.'

'Well, that's something.'

'What, that she's coming later or meeting with Spielberg?'

'That I can just sit here on my own for five minutes. The twittering round here is like a nightmare. Doesn't anyone ever sit still, or silent, in this town?'

'You are not actually on your own, you're with me. Would you like me to go away too?'

He studied her. Large chunks of ice clinked in thick glasses all around.

'Did you know,' he said, 'that now you are older your nose seems to have grown in proportion to your face? Or perhaps it is that your cheeks have sunk. When I first met you, I'll swear you had a little button nose like a doll. Now it's almost beaky.'

'I certainly feel less doll-like than I did twenty years ago,' she said. 'Do you like my dress?'

'Well, no. It's smart and silly. Isn't it too short?'

'No. Rowena Gersh helped me buy it. She said it was very LA. The style is casual, the fabric formal, everything matches and everyone is supposed to notice. Rowena Gersh, if you remember, is my agent, the one who's seeing Spielberg about a script of mine.'

'I hope she likes you. I see no evidence of it, from the dress. Or, God help us, the hat.'

'Hello. How are you today?' greeted another waiter, in passing. He had close-shaven white hair and a cavernous face, and brown, brown eyes. There seemed to be as many waiters as there were guests. All around arose the well-trained murmur; the formal acknowledgement that the rich deserve to be happy and content, not just in their bodies but in their minds as well, and that the poor must be considerate of the rich, not because the rich have money which the poor need so badly, but because the poor really *like* the rich. The rich are good guys and the poor are sweet guys. How are you? Have a nice day!

'I have worked out, Rix,' said Aileen, 'that the only reason we can go on calling women and blacks and Latinos and the underclass "minorities", although in actual numbers they overwhelm the majority ten times over, is that each minority soul is worth one-eleventh of each majority soul; only thus can the minority reasonably claim to be the majority. Powerful and strong the majority stands, spreading a little misery, a little kindness, complacently buffing its extra special soul.'

'Keep it for your agent,' he said. 'Couldn't you talk a little less? This is a very tense moment for me.'

Through the wide-open glass doors at the far end of the lounge bar of the brand-new Van Gogh hotel, past the central twelve-foot-high flower display, and the palms, and the silk screens, was the Leonardo Gallery, and here, in some half an hour, her husband's show would open.

'Night of the Private View,' she said. 'Always tense.' Disagreements had budded, blossomed, flourished and more or less faded. The paintings were finally unpacked and hung, the wall prices at last decided – $160,000 top price for a landscape fifteen feet by ten, $26,000 for a small flower piece and $15,000 – a snip – for a pencilled nude of fifteen, pregnant, which Aileen would rather he didn't sell, for fear of what the future might make of it, but hadn't ventured to say so. Mira Kaplan, who ran the gallery for Van Gogh International, had retired to her suite temporarily, to calm herself, and put on her new Armani suit, bought across the road in Rodeo Drive that very morning. Van Gogh International would no doubt foot the bill – a chain, recently developed, of 'Great Hotels of World Culture', anxious to launch themselves as just that, and lavishly scattering PR largesse. Rix, his paintings, and Aileen, his wife, as nursemaid, had been flown over from London six days earlier. Aileen was a screenwriter, as it happened. She had her own contacts in Los Angeles. Rix and Aileen seldom left home together.

'Hello,' greeted the white-haired waiter, returning. 'How are you today?' and he took out his notepad and held his pen between his thin, delicate brown fingers, because if these guys did not start focusing soon he would go off duty without bringing them their drink, or their coffee, or the cream cake of their fancy. He had sweet brown eyes. Aileen's eyes were blue; Rix's were grey. The waiter went away.

'Now you've missed your drink,' said Rix. 'It comes from talking too much.' He did not like the bland red wine of California, or the secret sweetness of its dry white Chardonnay. He seldom drank spirits. He liked to arrive at his Private Views sober, so as not to stumble or fall flat on his face in public, though he knew art buyers were not averse to a drunken, dissolute and ill-mannered artist. It made their connection with the churning heart of the universe the more poignant. He suspected the Van Gogh chain was part of an enormous world-wide conspiracy: its hotels mere clearing houses for Company Art, that is to say the big-scale, big-name, big-budget contemporary paintings which these days hung over board tables; from which the dealers profited so much, and the painters so little. It was gratifying to become one of the big names. It was also humiliating. To be successful, as a painter, was to have failed, to have been corrupted; the thin priest turning into the fat abbot. The trip to California was a mistake. He was not interested in establishing a reputation on the West Coast: he felt vulgar, and exposed. He didn't need the money. Aileen made enough money for them both anyway, writing rubbishy TV scripts.

He noticed that tears were rolling down Aileen's cheek. 'For God's sake,' he said, 'don't make an exhibition of yourself. Not here. I should have brought Frances, not you.' Frances was his sister. She too was a painter. She seldom spoke and never cried.

Aileen turned to look at him, and the cartwheel hat caught in her collar. She tugged it free.
'Somebody has asked me how I am today,' she said, 'and it has made me feel sorry for myself. Since there's no one else to tell and I finally have fifteen minutes to spare in which there is nothing I have to do, I shall tell you how I am. Why do I have fifteen minutes to spare? Because the Latinos are doing all the work for me. I am grateful to them. They are doing the cooking, the cleaning, the laundry, the taking of messages, the looking up of

maps to tell us where to go, the calling of cabs; a steady flow of reminder notes creeps under the door of our room upstairs, so I can empty my head of memory, and there is no justice in it, but in the three days I have been here I have had a little rest and I have seen how other women live, and how they live is *good*. Even the lonely ones who come and sit here at the Van Gogh in the afternoon on their own, with their expensive horrid clothes, and listen to the piano-player, who is young and romantic-looking, playing melancholy tunes which remind them of love past, and look so sad, so sad, are better off than I am.'

'You're wearing such expensive horrid clothes today,' he said.

'You know I hate spots and stripes.'

'That is why I went out this morning and bought this spotted dress,' she said. 'I went with Rowena.'

'You ought to go back to your therapist,' he said, 'in that case.'

'Don't interrupt me,' she said. 'I am telling you how I am. Hello, the waiter said. How are you today? And I know he is paid to say it, and trained to say it, but it got to my heart. Hello. How are you today?'

'You are drawing attention to yourself,' he said. 'Please don't.'

'I'll tell you something about yourself', she said, 'that you don't know. You don't know nothing from nix. You are a painter. You don't understand words. If you use them at all you use them as weapons. That to you is their only use. You and your sister are the same. You have a hereditary defect. You inherited it from your father because he was a painter too.'

'He was a bad painter.'

'You only remember the last sentence of any paragraph I speak because you are a painter, a visual person. Language flows through your brain; you don't pay it any attention, it is so unimportant: if there's any hanging about in your head when I've finished speaking you might just pay attention to it and respond. It does not matter whether your father was a bad painter or a good painter; indeed, it is because you are a painter, a visual artist, that you throw these concepts about so crudely. Good, bad. I see a whole world in between: of goodish and baddish and sometimes a little bit of both; you describe the painter, I describe the painting. I think you are childish.'

'You are doing your best', he said, 'to destroy this show for me.

You are so envious and jealous of my gift you want to attack me. You wait until now to do it.'

'You can always get up and walk away,' she said. 'But you won't because you'd rather people were talking about you than not talking about you and at this moment I am talking about you.'

'You don't know what you're talking about,' he said. 'You know nothing about me and you know nothing about painting and you make a fool of yourself pretending you do.'

'Hello,' she said. 'How are you today? Today I am speaking to my husband, that's how I am. I have been married to him for twenty-two years and I have never spoken to him properly, in case I spoke all this. I have had rows with him, and been unfaithful to him, and felt guilty, and he has left me and returned and had models for mistresses and mistresses for models and felt not at all guilty, and all these things have been overcome but I don't think this can be overcome now it has raised its head. You are a painter and a painter is a monster, no woman should marry an artist, because all artists are monsters, and very few men, you notice, marry women artists, being sensible, and if they do they do not survive. Or only as shells. They too serve art, whether they want to or not. All those who have sexual relations with artists serve art. The artist is the high priest, the spouse the acolyte, and acolytes, like the waiters who serve the priest which is money, who serves the god which is success, are sweet guys but have had the stuffing knocked out of them. A low self-image and a feeble sex drive. The wives of male artists pad round with ladders in their stockings; the husbands of female artists left long ago, or if they haven't, should have. It is a terrible thing for a man to have to revere art through his wife the artist: to thus funnel his soul through a woman is a humiliation. I am talking about your sister Frances and her husband Rex. She chose him for a husband because his name is Rex and yours is Rix, and it was the nearest she could get.'

'That old incest stuff again,' he said. 'Please keep your voice down.'

'And now Rex drinks and his face falls in folds, and he stumbles and trips and his eyes are bloodshot: and she, she is firm and determined and melancholy, and cold. She loves her art, she loves her painting: she could not ever love her children. She despises them. They disappoint her. They are not like a canvas she can work upon and work upon; they burst from her loins fully formed; no touch of cobalt blue, or stroke of titanium white, is going to make a difference. That's it, that's them: children are a puny creation compared to a painting. No woman artist truly loves her child. The child of the painter is the orphan of art. "Where is Mummy, Daddy?" "Mummy is in the studio, communing with her muse. Mummy has had a vision, darling. Mummy must communicate that vision to a world which doesn't know or care, and believes real is real, and knows that if you don't change a nappy the baby gets a nappy rash, but Mummy doesn't know that, or care, and the baby cries but all Mummy knows about is a vase of flowers which seem to her to have been sent as a message, to illuminate the world. As Jesus is to some, so is a landscape to a landscape artist; and God help the lambs who stumble round the real world because the artist sure as hell won't help them.'

'You don't know anything about these things,' he said. 'Why don't you stick to writing? Why don't you leave my unfortunate sister alone? Bad enough her losing the child without you capitalizing on it.'

'I am not capitalizing. I am observing. She was too busy painting to take the baby to the doctor. It was dreadful. I am not blaming her. I am trying to explain your own nature to you, using your sister, because you can see your sister just a little more clearly than you see yourself.'

'If I wanted to see myself clearly I would do a self-portrait.'

'You see, you see!' she cried in triumph, and finally took off her cartwheel hat, and her hair fell skewwhiff and she looked much more herself, he thought.

'It is a great blessing to be a painter and a great misfortune too. It is a blessing because you have a glimpse of a world behind this one, and a curse because you must try to seize it with tweezers, which are your brushes, like a splinter beneath flesh, and drag it into the day; if you do, it bruises and if you don't, it pains you if you press there by mistake, and if the pain doesn't stop, you know it's because the splinter is working its way, working its way inwards towards the heart and it will pierce the heart and you will die.'

'You know nothing about it, nothing.'

'And there is no one to talk to because your family and friends look at you as if you were mad, and your paintings are to them a mystery, a nuisance, and if they like them you despise them for having no taste, and if they don't you hate them, and you can't win: nor can you make up your mind if you are the worst painter in the world or the best, and all painters are the same in this; because painters are visual people and *see* good and bad, as kind of magnetic poles. They don't have any notion of the string hung like a washing line from pole to pole, on which paintings are pegged, ranged, at all stages between good and bad.'

'What are you talking about now? Washing lines?'

'And you want to talk to other painters but you daren't, in case they're laughing at you, despising your efforts: you share a secret with them but when you admit it you diminish that secret, because you acknowledge it as shared. So you get drunk with other painters, obliterate the mind, pick quarrels with them, say dreadful things about them behind their backs. They're your other family. But who wants to talk to family? You are intolerably lonely.'

'I wish I was alone, I can say that. I should never have asked you along.'

'You had to ask me along. You can't endure change. Only barely can you sit here in a foreign country. I am familiar, so you bring me with you. Here you are without your props. You exist in a visual world: even your peripheral vision is important. You know exactly how the light passes through the window at different times of day, and different seasons: when it's cloudy, when it's fine; as the sun rises, sinks. You have that degree of change taken into account. Only when it's black black thunderclouds are you thrown into disarray. You can't make sense of them. You haven't bargained for that natural blackness, in whatever pact you and your kind once made with the devil. You will come downstairs and pick a quarrel with me. I used to think it was electricity in the air that made you so bad-tempered and restless when there was thunder about: one day I understood it was just too sudden a change in the quality of light that affected your peripheral vision. It annoyed you. How can non-artists be expected to understand, let alone live with, artists? It is only because I love you that I have learned to do so,.that I put up with it.'

'Now she starts all that!' But his head was turned towards her.

'You are interested if I speak of my feelings for you,' she said, 'which is why I mention them. I hope you are picking up at least ten per cent of this.'

'Why do you always talk in percentages?' he asked. 'Figures are such cold and meaningless things.'

'I have to understand the world through my reason,' she said. 'I have to look beyond the evidence of my own eyes. You need only the evidence of yours: it is more than enough. So rich, it gives you indigestion.'

'In other words,' he said with satisfaction, 'you're blind. It has been a great handicap in my life, having to live with a blind woman. I should have married another artist.'

'Like your sister,' she said, but he replied, 'She was a lousy cook,' and even he could see this was outrageous, and he laughed, and so did she. For a moment they looked quite happy.

A waiter from the second shift approached them. He was of broader build than the one with the cropped white hair but his eyes were just as brown, soft and sweet.

'Hello,' he greeted them. 'And how are you today?'

'I'm very well,' she said brightly. 'I will have a spritzer and my husband will have a glass of water.' She liked to claim him, for all he was an artist.

'I hate it here,' he said. 'The glass, the perspex, the wealth, that ridiculous flowerpiece; it must be at least twelve feet high. Are the flowers real?'

'I think they grew,' she said, 'though possibly as the result of bioengineering.'

'Here even nature is perverted. Don't you notice that? How am I to do a flower painting ever again,' he said, averting his eyes, 'since the flowers themselves are man-made? This Private View is going to be a disaster. Nobody will come to it. Why should they? Californians aren't interested in painting.'

'Hello,' said a really smart Afro-Asian girl, with perfect skin, perfect features, and black hair briskly and firmly swept back from a wide clear brow. 'How are you today?' She seemed to be a manageress of some kind. She left behind her florets of raw cauliflower and long slivers of courgette prettily arranged in a glazed pottery dish, and went away without waiting for an answer.

'How I am today,' said Aileen to her husband, 'is how you are. When Jacob finally returned to the valley where his brother Esau lived, having made so many enemies that there was nowhere else to go, and remember how he had cheated and betrayed his brother and stolen his birthright, he made his wives walk before him, fearing Esau's attack. I feel like one of Jacob's wives, forever walking before you into danger, testing the water.'
'If I painted the girl who brought the vegetables,' was all Rix said, 'would it come out like Tretchikoff, who must be the richest painter in the world? You know the one – the girl with the green face and the flower behind her ear?'
'I know the one,' said Aileen, and waited for him to make some reference to Bill, her first husband years and years ago, an insurance agent, who in Rix's mind stood for everyone in the ordinary world, both philistine and fascist, but he didn't. He just said, 'I'm sure you do.'

'How I am is how you are,' she said. 'And, another thing, you are superstitious, and both our lives are narrowed by that superstition. You are superstitious about how you work, where you work. You must have certain brushes, laid out in a certain order, a certain number of tubes of titanium white in reserve; and each must be just so, the leaf-fringed window of the studio to the left, the old yellow sofa to the right. I understand you. You hate me to understand you but I do. You stopped painting altogether for many years; on the day you started again the brushes were laid out just so; the window was there, the sofa was here; and lo, it worked. The muse descended. The magic returned. It seemed to you such a miracle, such a heavenly coming together of events and circumstances, that ever since you've been frightened to alter any of the ingredients in case the whole thing falls apart again, in case the magic stops working. You have, alas, included the window and the sofa in the jigsaw, so now we hardly ever go away, or you hate it when we do, and we can't have the sofa cleaned and it is filthy beyond belief, but part of the gestalt you depend upon. The sofa has become a sacred object. You can just about tolerate the way the creeper loses its leaves in winter, that being according to nature not man, but if you could prevent it you would – intercede with God to alter the seasons just so you could paint your vision out.

'But you are stronger than you think; or rather your art is. You could paint anywhere and it would work; even in our hotel room upstairs, but no, you would rather brood upon your own fragility: build up your own self-importance, see yourself as the message, and not what you are, merely a messenger. The instrument, not the music itself. You and your dirty old sofa. Throw it out the window: chop the creeper down at its mouldy old root. It would make no difference.'

'I know you can write anywhere,' he said. 'But painting is not writing.'

'Not so different as you think,' she said. A waiter, unnoticed, had brought them their drinks. In hers stood a glass spike, for mixing. When she drank, it all but pierced her eye.

'If you were blind,' he observed, 'you could still write. You would dictate.'

Waiters began to carry trays of glasses through to the Gallery. Boxes of wine were already stacked by the white-sheeted tables. More staff arrived to clear the far part of the lounge-bar to create an extra annexe. It looked as if they expected a crush. They ran around with the tall palms in their ornate pots and the elaborate silk screens, and Aileen watched through and around them in the distance the shifting shapes of oranges and ochres of her husband's paintings. They seemed to her, even seen like this, through change and confusion, to have a validity, a right to exist, more intense than anything else the world offered. Mira appeared, tiny and thin and smart and no longer young, to beckon them through. They followed her. The first guests were arriving: bangles clanked and tanned and handsome faces glowed.

'I'm fine, I'm fine,' they greeted one another. The high ceiling echoed to their fineness. Aileen and Rix paused together in the glass doorway.

'Oh well,' said Aileen, 'I'm on your side really. This is going to be terrible. The only thing that really worries me, is that though

how I am is how you are, how you are is nothing whatsoever to
do with how I am.'
'Exactly,' he said. 'Me being a painter and you being a writer.'

She thought about this for a little, and observing how smart
little Mira Kaplan came hurrying back to collect him, and how
possessively the red fingernails were laid upon his arm, decided to
leave her to it, and indeed him, and turned and went upstairs to
pack. She would go and stay with Rowena Gersh for a long, long
time.

TALES OF THE NEW AGE

Down the Clinical Disco

You never know where you'll meet your own true love. I met mine down the clinical disco. That's him over there, the thin guy with the jeans, the navy jumper and the red woolly cap. He looks pretty much like anyone else, don't you think? That's hard work on his part, not to mention mine, but we got there in the end. Do you want a drink? Gin? Tonic? Fine. I'll just have an orange juice. I don't drink. Got to be careful. You never know who's watching. They're everywhere. Sorry, forget I said that. Even a joke can be paranoia. Do you like my hair? That's a golden gloss rinse. Not my style really: I have this scar down my cheek: see, if I turn to the light? A good short crop is what suits me best, always has been: I suppose I've got what you'd call a strong face. Oops, sorry, dear, didn't mean to spill your gin; it's the heels. I do my best but I can never quite manage stilettos. But it's an ill wind; anyone watching would think I'm ever so slightly tipsy, and that's normal, isn't it. It is not absolutely A-okay not to drink alcohol. On the obsessive side. *Darling, of course there are people watching*.

Let me tell you about the clinical disco while Eddie finishes his game of darts. He hates darts but darts are what men do in pubs, okay? The clinical disco is what they have once a month at Broadmoor. (Yes, that place. Broadmoor. The secure hospital for the criminally insane.) You didn't know they had women there? They do. One woman to every nine men. They often don't look all that like women when they go in but they sure as hell look like them when (and if, if, if, if, if, if) they go out.

How did I get to be in there? You really want to know? I'd been having this crummy time at home and this crummy time at work. I was pregnant and married to this guy I loved, God knows why, in retrospect, but I did, only he fancied my mother, and he got her pregnant too – while I was out at work – did you know women can get pregnant at fifty? He didn't, she didn't, I didn't – but she was! My mum said he only married me to be near her anyway and I was the one who ought to have an abortion. So I did. It went wrong and messed me up inside, so I couldn't have babies, and my mum said what did it matter, I was a lesbian anyway, just look at me. I got the scar in a road accident, in case you're wondering. And I thought what the hell, who wants a man, who wants a mother, and walked out on them. And I was working at the Royal Opera House for this man who was a real pain, and you know how these places get: the dramas and the rows and the overwork and the underpay and the show must go on though you're dropping dead. Dropping dead babies. No, I'm not crying. What do you think I am, a depressive? I'm as normal as the next person.

What I did was set fire to the office. Just an impulse. I was having these terrible pains and he made me work late. He said it was my fault Der Rosenkavalier's wig didn't fit: he said I'd made his opera house a laughing stock: the wig slipped and the *New York Times* noticed and jeered. But it wasn't my fault about the wig: wardrobe had put the message through to props, not administration. And I sat in front of the VDU – the union is against them: they cause infertility in women but what employer's going to worry about a thing like that – they'd prefer everyone childless any day – and thought about my husband and my mum, five months pregnant, and lit a cigarette. I'd given up smoking for a whole year but this business at home had made me start again. Have you ever had an abortion at five months? No? Not many have.

How's your drink? How's Eddie getting on with the darts? Started another game? That's A-okay, that's fine by me, that's normal.

So what were we saying, Linda? Oh yes, arson. That's what they called it. I just moved my cigarette lighter under the curtains and they went up, whoosh, and they caught some kind of soundproof ceiling infill they use these days instead of plaster. Up it all went.

Whoosh again. Four hundred pounds' worth of damage. Or so they said. If you ask me, they were glad of the excuse to redecorate.

Like a fool, instead of lying and just saying it was an accident, I said I'd done it on purpose, I was glad I had, opera was a waste of public funds, and working late a waste of my life. That was before I got to court. The solicitor laddie warned me off. He said arson was no laughing matter, they came down very hard on arson. I thought a fine, perhaps: he said no, prison. Years not months.

You know my mum didn't even come to the hearing? She had a baby girl. I thought there might be something wrong with it, my mum being so old, but there wasn't. Perhaps the father being so young made up for it.

There was a barrister chappie. He said look you've been upset, you are upset, all this business at home. The thing for you to do is plead insane; we'll get you sent to Broadmoor, it's the best place in the country for psychiatric care, they'll have you right in the head in no time. Otherwise it's Holloway, and that's all strip cells and major tranquillizers, and not so much of a short sharp shock as a long sharp shock. Years, it could be, arson.

So that's what I did, I pleaded insane, and got an indefinite sentence, which meant into Broadmoor until such time as I was cured and safe to be let out into the world again. I never was unsafe. You know what one of those famous opera singers said when she heard what I'd done? 'Good for Philly,' she said. 'Best thing that could possibly happen: the whole place razed to the ground.' Only of course it wasn't razed to the ground, there was just one room already in need of redecoration slightly blackened. When did I realize I'd made a mistake? The minute I saw Broadmoor: a great black pile: the second I got into this reception room. There were three women nurses in there, standing around a bath of hot water; great hefty women, and male nurses too, and they were talking and laughing. Well, not exactly laughing, but an Inside equivalent; a sort of heavy grunting ha-ha-ha they manage, halfway between sex and hate. They didn't even look at me as I came in. I was terrified, you can imagine. One of them said 'strip' over her shoulder and I just stood there not believing it. So she barked 'strip' again, so I took off a cardigan and my shoes, and then one of them just ripped everything off me and pushed my legs apart and yanked out a Tampax – sorry about this, Linda – and threw it in a bin and dunked me in the bath without even seeing me. Do you know what's worse than being naked and seen by strangers, including men strangers? It's being naked and unseen, because you don't even count as a woman. Why men? In case the women patients are uncontrollable. The bath was dirty. So were the nurses. I asked for a sanitary towel but no one replied. I don't know if they were being cruel: I don't think they thought that what came out of my mouth were words. Well I was mad, wasn't I? That's why I was there. I was mad because I was a patient, I was wicked because I was a prisoner: they were sane because they were nurses and good because they could go home after work.

Linda, is that guy over there in the suit watching? No? You're sure?

They didn't go far, mind you, most of them. They lived, breathed, slept The Hospital. Whole families of nurses live in houses at the foot of the great Broadmoor wall. They intermarry. Complain about one and you find you're talking to the cousin, aunt, lover or best friend of the complainee. You learn to shut up: you learn to smile. I was a tea bag for the whole of one day and I never stopped smiling from dawn to dusk. That's right, I was a tea bag. Nurse Kelly put a wooden frame round my shoulders and hung a piece of gauze front and back and said 'You be a tea bag all day' so I was. How we all laughed. Why did he want me to be a tea bag? It was his little joke. They get bored, you see. They look to the patients for entertainment.

Treatment? Linda, I saw one psychiatrist six times and I was there three years. The men do better. They have rehabilitation programmes, ping-pong, carpentry and we all get videos. Only the men get to choose the video and they always choose blue films. They have to choose them to show they're normal, and the women have to choose not to see them to show the same. You have to be normal to get out. Sister in the ward fills in the report cards. She's the one who decides whether or not you're sane enough to go before the Parole Committee. The trouble is, she's not so sane herself. She's more institutionalized than the patients.

Eddie, come and join us! How was your game? You won? Better not do that too often. You don't want to be seen as an over-achiever. This is Linda, I'm telling her how we met. At the clinical disco. Shall we do a little dance, just the pair of us, in the middle of everything and everyone, just to celebrate being out? No, you're right, that would be just plain mad. Eddie and I love each other, Linda, we met at the clinical disco, down Broadmoor way. Who knows, the doctor may have been wrong about me not having babies; stranger things happen. My mum ran out on my ex, leaving him to look after the baby: he came to visit me in Broadmoor once and asked me to go back to him, but I wouldn't. Sister put me back for that: a proper woman wants to go back to her husband, even though he's her little sister's father. And after he'd gone I cried. You must never cry in Broadmoor. It means you're depressed; and that's the worst madness of all. The staff all love it in there, and think you're really crazy if you don't. I guess they get kind of offended if you cry. So it's on with the lipstick and smile, smile, smile, though everyone around you is ballooning with largactyl and barking like the dogs they think they are.

I tell you something, Linda, these places are mad-houses. Never, never plead the balance of your mind is disturbed in court: get a prison sentence and relax, and wait for time to pass and one day you'll be free. Once you're in a secure hospital, you may never get out at all, and they fill the women up with so many tranquillizers, you may never be fit to. The drugs give you brain damage. But I reckon I'm all right; my hands tremble a bit, and my mouth twitches sometimes, but it's not too bad. And I'm still *me*, aren't I. Eddie's fine – they don't give men so much, sometimes none at all. Only you never know what's in the tea. But you can't be seen not drinking it, because that's paranoia.

Eddie says I should sue the barrister, with his fine talk of therapy and treatment in Broadmoor, but I reckon I won't. Once you've been in you're never safe. They can pop you back inside if you cause any trouble at all, and they're the ones who decide what trouble is. So we keep our mouths shut and our noses clean, we ex-inmates of Broadmoor.

Are you sure that man's not watching? Is there something wrong with us? Eddie? You're not wearing your earring, are you? Turn your head. No, that's all right. We look just like everyone else. Don't we? Is my lipstick smudged? Christ, I hate wearing it. It makes my eyes look small.

At the clinical disco! They hold them at Broadmoor every month. Lots of the men in there are sex offenders, rapists, mass murderers, torturers, child abusers, flashers. The staff like to see how they're getting on, how they react to the opposite sex, and on the morning of the disco Sister turns up and says 'you go' and 'you' and 'you' and of course you can't say no, no matter how scared you are. Because you're supposed to want to dance. And the male staff gee up the men – hey, look at those titties! Wouldn't you like to look up *that* skirt – and stand by looking forward to the trouble, a bit of living porno, better than a blue film any day. And they gee up the women too: wow, there's a handsome hunk of male: and you have to act interested, because that's normal: if they think you're a lezzie you never get out. And the men have to act interested, but not too interested. Eddie and I met at the clinical disco, acting just gently interested. Eddie felt up my titties, and I rubbed myself against him and the staff watched and all of a sudden he said 'Hey, I mean really,' and I said 'Hi,' and he said 'Sorry about this, keep smiling,' and I said, 'Ditto, what are you in for?' and he said 'I got a job as a woman teacher. Six little girls framed me. But I love teaching, not little girls. There was just no job for a man,' and I believed him: nobody else ever had. And I told him about my mum and my ex, and he seemed to understand. Didn't you, Eddie! That's love, you see. Love at first sight. You're just on the other person's side, and if you can find someone else like that about you, everything falls into place. We were both out in three months. It didn't matter for once if I wore lipstick, it didn't matter to him if he had to watch blue films: you stop thinking that acting sane is driving you mad: you don't have not to cry because you stop wanting to cry: the barking and howling and screeching stop worrying you; I guess when you're in love you're just happy so they have to turn you out; because your being happy shows them up. If you're happy, what does sane or insane mean, what are their lives all about? They can't bear to see it.

Linda, it's been great meeting you. Eddie and I are off home now. I've talked too much. Sorry. When we're our side of our front door I scrub off the make-up and get into jeans and he gets into drag, and we're ourselves, and we just hope no one comes knocking on the door to say, hey that's not normal, back to Broadmoor, but I reckon love's a talisman. If we hold on to that we'll be okay.

Pumpkin Pie

This is a story for Thanksgiving. Pay good attention or there won't be many more – and I mean Thanksgivings, not stories. The rich have got to come to some accommodation with the poor – and by that I don't mean provide housing (though I can see that might help) but 'to accommodate' in its old sense: that is to say recognize, come towards, incorporate, compromise.

Otherwise, I tell you, next year or the year after, there'll be poison in the packet of mix for the pumpkin piecrust and not only that: some person will step out of the shadows and knife you as you stop your car for once outside, not inside, your high-security garage, the better to take the giant pumpkin for the filling out of the boot. That person will be your conscience. How much do you think they paid the man who grew the pumpkin? Enough to live on? Enough to pay a doctor to get the pesticide out of his lungs? Of course not. Are you still listening? Or have you turned the music up? One of the things you should never do in the presence of the rich, I know, is to mention the problems of the poor. It is in the worst possible taste. Almost as bad as suggesting to the rich that that is what they are – rich. Well, it's understandable. The hearts of the rich bleed for the poor, of course they do, but what can they do about any of it? Bleed to death?

Look, I don't want you to share your pumpkin pie. The poor make pumpkin pie just as well as the rich – given a sink, of course, an oven, some ingredients and a scrap of energy left over from survival – and probably make it better, usually belonging to some immigrant community in which the tradition of home-cooking still lives. This is no compensation for being poor, mind you. I am not of Solzhenitsyn's opinion, when he reckoned that the piece of dry bread saved against all the odds by Ivan Denisovitch in the labour camp tasted better than a rich man's feast. No.

Take Antoinette for example. Antoinette was the maid up at the Marvin household. The Marvins were once of banker stock but now owned shopping malls and theme parks in the West. They weren't particularly *nouveau riche* or vulgar: they had books on the shelves, and a good painting or two on the walls, and the ballgames stayed silent on the giant screens all through Thanksgiving dinner. The house was on many levels, true, with an indoor swimming pool and a workout room full of wonderful metallic shapes, and thin elegant trees growing through glass tables as if indoors were the same as out; and it was built for the family by the family, custom-built with an eye for detail, and it had high steel fences and a barred steel gate which slid aside gracefully for known and named guests, and kept the poor, the hungry and the angry out. This year Thanksgiving dinner was to be buffet-style, that is to say eaten on the lap not around the table. Antoinette's family – she had raised seven children without benefit of live-in or maintaining husband – would not have thanked her for requiring them to eat their food on their laps. But Honey Marvin, who liked everything just perfect, had decided that was how Thanksgiving would be – a buffet. Sit-down dinners were old-fashioned and clumsy, and her husband, John Junior, might take the opportunity to eat and drink too much, against the nutritionist's advice. Antoinette and Claire, the Cordon Bleu girl, could surely manage a buffet; only eleven guests this year anyway, which with family meant thirteen – thirteen; that really got Honey going: it took both her familiar psychiatrist and her new fortune-teller to calm her down about thirteen. Sometimes Honey confessed to guests that she'd really rather not entertain at all: she couldn't endure it: you either asked the wrong people, or you forgot one or other of the right people; and John Junior would sulk, and not say a word to anyone, or John Junior would not sulk, and say too much. She would make the cranberry sauce herself and everything else would be home-made by the staff.

So there would be no day off for Antoinette. Antoinette knew better than to ask: asking would be spoiling the spirit of the occasion. It wasn't all bad – she would be allowed to take home the leftovers and there would be plenty, twice as much as anyone could possibly need because Honey Marvin was like that. Well, not exactly 'allowed to take home' – she would be presented with a basket of prettily wrapped cold turkey legs (Texas the guard dog was hand-fed the white meat) and cold sweet-potato patties.

'Oh thank you, ma'am. Isn't that real pretty!'

'But we're so obliged to you, Antoinette. What would we do without you? You're part of the family. Here, you're forgetting the chocolate-chip cookies. Don't dream of leaving the chocolate-chip cookies behind!'

Ma'am was always desperate to get the cookies out of the house: otherwise she might succumb and eat them and then she'd have to do an extra couple of hours' workout penance. She was as thin as a praying mantis; hold up her mean little hand to the light and you could see right through it; if she ate anything not Pritikin the whole meaning of her life was gone. She'd have hysterics if there was a drop of oil in the lemon dressing on the spinach salad, yet sometimes whole walnut cakes would vanish from the fridge overnight, and that couldn't be John Junior because since his operation John Junior only got about in a wheelchair and anyway since John Junior Marvin's operation the fridge was a special new make with a lock on it and Honey Marvin had the key. Honey Marvin just threw the old fridge out: Antoinette would have liked it but she wasn't going to ask. It would have been too tall for her kitchen, of course, but she could have put it on its side, or in the yard. Mr Junior had had a triple bypass three months back and now finally Honey had him eating the way she did, though sometimes John Junior fought back, as well as a man in a wheelchair can fight back. Antoinette was sorry for him but not all that sorry.

Antoinette took out the family silver for Thanksgiving and hand-polished it as Honey Marvin wanted her to do, though it had been done when she put it away after the summer party, and wrapped in tissue since then, but there you were, that was Honey Marvin for you. Things had to be done just right. Honey Marvin spent $500 on an all-white table centrepiece, then decided she hated it, threw it in pieces round the room, changed decorators, and got in a centrepiece which cost $1,250. She didn't like that one either but said she wasn't going to waste any more money on stupid things like centrepieces when bits of old tree would do.

'What do you think, Antoinette? You must *have* thoughts.'

'I think it's real pretty, ma'am.'

'It's certainly very bright, if that's what you mean. Well, they're the in decorators. God knows why.'

And then everything in the dining room had to be changed; the pale furniture moved out to the rumpus room: the strong-coloured pieces from the covered patio brought in to match the centrepiece, and still it wasn't right. Hired movers and cleaners came and went. Then Claire called the day before Thanksgiving to say she was sick and was fired on the spot for lack of loyalty and love: she'd posted a doctor's certificate from Honey's own physician – crawled to the post with it, or so she said – but it was Claire's manner on the phone which really upset Honey. Which meant Antoinette had to do all the cooking, even the cranberry sauce because Honey's hand developed neuralgia, she was under such a strain; and at Thanksgiving you really can't use caterers. Apart from anything else, they'd cheat. They wouldn't keep everything cholesterol-free. Especially the pumpkin pie. For cholesterol-free pumpkin pie you use a fat-free crust and the filling's made with white of egg, not whole of egg.

And meanwhile, at home, Cheri, Antoinette's nineteen-year-old married daughter, the one who'd just had a C-section baby, had turned up weeping with a black eye. Her husband's parents had said she should go back to work straight away and she'd said she couldn't, she was weak from the operation, and the debts were mounting up; but they were so young, the pair of them. Antoinette knew if she could just *talk* to them – but she had to be at work by six to get the turkey in the oven so it could be cold enough for supper because one of Honey's friends had read you should never chill a turkey in the fridge, only at room temperature. Fortunately Honey Marvin didn't have many friends. Antoinette had noticed this. She'd have guests, but they weren't what Antoinette would call friends. Honey gave them a lot of presents, tiny little things, silver or gold, cute, beautifully wrapped. Antoinette had at one time saved the paper and smoothed it and taken it home for the kids to make collages with, but she'd had a memo from Mr Marvin's office to all staff saying 'no domestic accoutrements, even when apparently discarded, were to be removed from the dwelling', which she and Juanita next door had finally deciphered as meaning Honey didn't like her taking the paper home and she'd better stop or else. Honey never raised her voice or got mad at you; she was the sweetest thing. Everyone said so, especially John Junior. Well, he had to. He was trapped. He didn't speak too well, either. Antoinette reckoned he'd had a stroke as well as a bypass but no one was saying. Sometimes Honey flipped and someone got fired, and stayed fired, but mostly she spoke soft and memos got sent from the office.

That's enough of that. You get the picture? Whose side are you on, I wonder? The employers or the hired help? The rich or the poor? Have I loaded the scales? No. You wish I had, but I haven't. Who are you identifying with? Honey Marvin, Antoinette, Cheri's husband, or John Junior? A bit of all of them? I hope so. That way progress lies. If it hurts, it heals.

Anyway, this Thanksgiving there was Antoinette working a sixteen-hour day worried stiff about Cheri – though at least Juanita was helping with the baby, her first grandchild – and the two boys still at home – thirteen and fourteen – would have to move over and share a bed and she was not there to handle any of it, keep things smooth, she even wondered if she should call off sick too, but if she was fired, then what? They stuck together, the ladies who lived in big houses, the kind which had steel doors to let you into the property, remotely controlled from the house. They'd call Honey and Honey would say, 'She just wasn't into the spirit of the household. She let me down when I needed her most,' and then what could Antoinette do? A dumpy 45-year-old Latino with a scar down the side of her face, so she needed to keep to the kitchen, wasn't right for opening doors and smiling? If she had time she'd get herself to college and learn English properly, but with seven kids and Honey Marvin what could she do? And now Cheri was back with baby Gerry, who was cute; and if they wanted to stay they'd have to stay. Who could afford housing?

Antoinette had the turkey in the slow oven – basted in yoghurt, not oil – and the cholesterol-free pumpkin pie in the fast oven. She gave the stripped turkey skin (the fat in poultry is always just beneath the skin) to Texas the guard dog to calm him down: if he got hungry he was likely to bite: she'd had to have stitches twice and was now known as 'not good with Texas'. Honey Marvin liked a spotless kitchen whenever she walked into it, so Antoinette kept the pots and pans cleaned up as she went.

Honey Marvin walked in and said, 'You are a treasure, Antoinette, coping with thirteen single-handed; why have you taken your shoes off? We have to be so careful about hygiene, what with Mr Marvin's special requirements. Please put them on again.' So Antoinette did, though they hurt in a way that soft leather shoes don't; and just as well, because Texas squatted and crapped there and then, as he often did when Honey Marvin came in. Honey Marvin needed Texas to protect her at night in her great big house on many levels – now that John Junior slept soundly at last, on sleeping pills – but she'd have done without him if she could. She just ignored him and walked out, so Antoinette cleared it up.

Honey Marvin came back presently and said, 'I remember now. There's a phone call for you on the rumpus-room extension. Don't be too long. It's Thanksgiving, after all, and John Junior and I are calling all our friends and family and the lines are busy,' though the red light on the extension in the kitchen which meant the phones were in use hadn't shown all morning. Antoinette went to the rumpus-room phone and Juanita said, 'I thought you'd never come. Get home quick, Antoinette, your Cheri's husband is banging on the door and she's in here crying and he's going to murder us all.'

So Antoinette gave Texas the bowl of six left-over egg yolks to keep him quiet and just ran from the big house, out the back door, through the garage with the ten cars so squashed in that no one could ever get any but two of them out, and she squeezed through the hole in the fence everyone but the Marvins knew about, and ran for ten minutes solid to get home, and when she did found

Cheri and her husband sobbing and smiling and sighing in each other's arms, and she was glad because she liked the young man, he was just so young, and a baby needs two parents, and the smell of a pumpkin pie which the boys were making was rich and strong in the house, and there was Juanita saying she was sorry, she was sorry, she'd got frightened, and Antoinette grabbed the hot pumpkin pie out of the oven because she knew the one at the Marvins' would be burned, she'd forgotten to turn the oven down, and the boys said that's okay, that's okay, because they were good kids, and she borrowed six eggs from Juanita who, what with the bangings and crashings, hadn't got round to making her own, and ran back to the house, and she was in through the hole in the fence and sure enough the kitchen was full of the smell of burnt, fat-free, egg-yolk-free pumpkin pie but she switched on all the extractor fans, of which there were many, and whisked the ruined pie out of the oven, burning her fingers so she dropped it on the floor and it skidded under the table and Texas ate it, as she knew he would, scalding his mouth but he didn't care.

'That's a good-looking pumpkin pie,' said Honey Marvin, staring at the one Antoinette had brought from home, one second after the evidence had been eaten, 'but what's that funny smell? It didn't burn, did it?' If there was anything Honey Marvin hated it was the waste of burned food, of food caught on the bottoms of the very best pans.

'Don't look like burned to me, ma'am,' said Antoinette, and though Honey Marvin peered and peered she couldn't see a speck of burned pastry, and one pumpkin pie looks much like another, whether you're rich or whether you're poor.

'That was a *very* good pumpkin pie,' said Honey Marvin at ten o'clock that evening, when she came in to lock the fridge and Antoinette was on her hands and knees cleaning the kitchen floor. (You can only clean a floor properly on your hands and knees, as Honey Marvin's friends declared.) 'You didn't put egg yolk in it, did you? Because, as you know, egg yolk can kill my husband.'

'Why, ma'am, here's the proof no egg yolk went into that pumpkin pie,' said Antoinette, showing Honey Marvin a bowl with six of Juanita's egg yolks in it – Texas had turned up his nose at the whites, as she knew he would, but there was no harm trying. So she'd put them down the waste.

'Antoinette,' said Honey Marvin, 'I know you're loyal and true to us, and here's a little Thanksgiving gift to prove it,' and gave her a little silver salt-cellar one of her friends had upset her by not accepting because these days the rich can't eat salt, it's so full of sodium; the friend had actually stamped and left in a fury, crying 'Honey Marvin, you're nothing but a murdering bitch' but then Thanksgiving is like that sometimes, everyone knows.

'Thank you kindly, ma'am,' said fat Antoinette, podgy Antoinette, scarred Antoinette, good Antoinette, who salted her food and ate real pumpkin pie and didn't care one bit whether Honey Marvin's husband lived or died, and would you? And she went home to her family at last, barefoot, because her feet hurt, and they'd all given up waiting and gone to sleep. And she was glad. She put her head on her pillow and slept too.

The moral of this Thanksgiving story is not that the poor are happier than the rich. They're not. But that the only point in being rich, as the palate of the wealthy gets jaded, lies in not being poor. The rich do what they can to make the poor *mind* being poor to keep the differential going. And the poor do mind, and they consent to being poor less and less, and there are more and more of them about. Had you noticed? And they begin to know that the pumpkin pies of the poor taste as good if not better than the pumpkin pies of the rich; so if you can't make your own, do without, and let the hired help stay home for a change. Or you'll find cholesterol in your pie and a knife in your back, and a good thing too.

See the drop of blood upon the page? That's mine. That's just the beginning.

Sharon Loves Darren

'Sharon,' said Nurse Emily Fitt, patiently, 'now, Sharon, if you don't swallow this tube, you will die.'

'Want to die,' said Sharon. And then she called her lover's name aloud, so that the sound bounced back from pale-green walls, up and down the casualty cubicles, softened by stacked cardboard boxes (labelled 'Cardiac Infibulation', or 'Tracheotomy', or 'Paediatric Artery' or whatever) but sharpened by racks of stainless steel, upon which were stacked instruments for the cutting and closing of human flesh.

'Darren! Oh Darren, save me!'

'Look,' said Nurse Emily Fitt, who wore a badge claiming 'a legend in her time' on her tidy uniform, and whose face was neat and intelligent and composed – she was all of twenty-four – 'Look Sharon, just swallow this tube or you'll go into liver failure and die. Do you understand?' But all Sharon did was shriek for Darren again and then clamp her mouth shut against the intrusive poking pale-yellow tube. Sharon was seventeen. She wore laddered black tights and a bra. They'd stripped her of everything else. She'd drunk a bottle of sherry, a bottle of whisky and a bottle of wine during the course of the evening, and taken twenty-five paracetamol tablets, a whole bottleful, for love of Darren, who had taken Debbie to the cinema instead of her.

Darren was nineteen, and sitting out in the waiting room, reading the sports page of last Saturday's *Sun*. I'd noticed him earlier when I took my turn to wait for attention. He had acne and cropped pale-reddish hair. What he thought it was impossible to tell. He did not stir. If Sharon's voice had reached him he was deaf to it. Or perhaps it just bored him. He'd heard it too often.

'Sharon,' said Nurse Fitt, 'we want to help you but if you don't make an effort yourself we can't.'

I lay in the next cubicle, in no urgent medical need, and listened. The curtains between us were open. Sharon went into fits of bitter weeping. 'Oh Darren, Darren, my heart is breaking.' I believed her. I'd cried like that myself, in my time.

Sister Radice, all bosom and big dark eyes, fetched me a cup of tea. I was privileged. I had responded to medical treatment and could now be sent home. I was waiting to be fetched. 'These girls,' she murmured, 'they don't know how dangerous paracetamol is. They take it by the handful. We do our best but sometimes they don't make it. I blame the drug companies.'

'Oh, Darren, Darren,' cried Sharon, lovesick Sharon, and tears came to my own eyes.

'I want to go to the loo,' yelled Sharon, suddenly, furiously, like the spoilt and naughty child she was.

'Not yet, not yet,' said she who was a legend in her own time, 'it can wait. Just swallow the tube.'

'It can't wait,' said her patient nastily. 'What am I supposed to do, wet my pants?'

'Better than dying,' said Nurse Emily, but Sharon didn't agree.

'Leave me alone,' Sharon begged, 'leave me to die.'

'Look,' said Nurse Emily, who was little more than a child herself, but at least was sensible, 'if you die your parents will go mad.'

'They're mad already,' said Sharon, cunningly. 'They hate Darren anyway.'

'Not surprised,' muttered Emily Fitt. 'So do I.'

Sharon's sick soaked into a newspaper on the floor. They'd made her vomit when the ambulance came in; given her an emetic before she'd had time to protest. The young doctor (Dr Angus Love, according to his lapel badge, but how could one be sure? Perhaps they made their names up?) had poked through the mess, fish and chips swirling round in sherry, whisky and wine, but only found four paracetamol tablets, half-disintegrated, which meant there were another twenty-one left inside her. She'd have to be stomach-pumped, but a conscious patient, when it comes to it, is more difficult than one in a coma. He'd left the job to Emily. He was busy. Everyone was.

'I say,' said Sharon, plaintively, between shrieks and sobs. 'I feel rather sick.'

'I expect you do,' said Emily Fitt. 'Sick to death. Swallow the tube!'

'You want to hurt me.'

'We don't want to hurt you. Why should we want to hurt you?'

'Because you don't like me,' said Sharon, acutely. 'Because I love Darren! Darren, save me! Let me see Darren. Please, let me see Darren.'

'No,' said Nurse Emily Fitt, and the department filled again with the sound of Sharon's noisy distress, and Sharon's furious little laddered and holed foot banged against the partition wall and saline drips everywhere trembled and faltered, and heart monitors, over-sensitive, gave perfectly absurd readings.

'I love Darren. I want to die for Darren!' cried Sharon.

'Just shut up, will you,' said Nurse Emily. 'If you think I haven't better things to do than look after you, you're mistaken. There are children in casualty. You're scaring them to death carrying on like this. You don't want to frighten little children, do you?'

'I love Darren,' shrieked Sharon. 'Fetch me Darren, you bitch!'

'Swallow the tube.'

'No. Wont.'

'Die then,' said Nurse Emily Fitt, and she went off to attend to a heart attack (or so he feared) and a young woman with an abscess on her Fallopian tube (or so she said, and she was certainly grim and white with pain and would swallow anything at all, even poison, to put a stop to it). I was formally discharged.

'Goodbye,' said Nurse Emily Fitt, cheerfully, escorting me to the door.

'Look,' I said, 'tell her if she dies Debbie will get Darren.'

'That's an idea,' said Nurse Emily, but I didn't think she was going to go back and say any such thing. I had a feeling that if young Dr Love didn't return quite promptly from the broken back (I'd heard them. Mother of three, drunk, backwards out of a first-floor window. The doctor, slowly and clearly: 'Mrs Able, do you understand? Try to listen. You are in hospital. You fell out of a window and have broken your back. We are admitting you') to look in on Sharon, she would simply go into liver failure and die, and Nurse Emily would be busy elsewhere, and Sister Radice would break the news to Darren, who would look up from the sports page and be quite astonished, if so strong an emotion were available to him, which I rather doubted, at what could happen if you took Debbie to the cinema one Sunday night, instead of Sharon.

STORIES FOR CHRISTMAS

Who Goes Where?

A CHRISTMAS TALE

'No!' said Adrienne. You know how some children are when they're four?
'Put on your nice new coat, please?'
'No!'
'Look, a spoonful of this lovely apple mousse?'
'No!'
'Adrienne, darling, please.'
'No!'
Little arms stiff, little mouth clamped shut against the world, exercising the power of the much-loved over the one who loves and is thus humiliated. Except that Adrienne was thirty-four, not four, and still doing it, as only the really beautiful can, but nearer to running out of people who loved her than she knew. Or perhaps she didn't care.

She'd always been like that. Sometimes people forgot, and asked, 'Adrienne, can I borrow your pink shoes to go to the ball?'
'No!'
'Adrienne, could you give me a job to help me out?'
'No!'
'Adrienne, your grandma's ill, will you visit her?'
'No!'
'Adrienne, will you please stop sleeping with Cynthia's husband?'
'No!'

What Adrienne had – beautiful clothes – Adrienne didn't share. What Adrienne had won – worldly success – Adrienne took care to keep. What Adrienne didn't want – like grandmothers – Adrienne abandoned. What Adrienne wanted, like Cynthia's husband Tyro,

95

she got. Though quite what Adrienne saw in Tyro, whom Cynthia until then had thought was rather ordinary, indeed if anything rather incompetent and messy, Cynthia couldn't at first work out. Perhaps Cynthia's opinion of Tyro, in those early days, and her impatience with him, were why Tyro became obsessed with Adrienne, why Adrienne could just pluck him, twist him off the family branch, and there he was, in her hand, ripe and ready, smartened up and polished and writing music for major feature films, no longer just a struggling session hack. You never know what you've got till it's gone and once Tyro had gone Cynthia and the three children wept and wept.

'No!' said Adrienne when, five years after her marriage to Tyro, Cynthia asked if Adrienne could take the children, Alec aged ten, Alison aged eight, and Edward aged six, for Christmas Day. They wanted to have their Christmas presents at home and go to their father for Christmas dinner. And she, Cynthia, had been asked out somewhere special . . .
'No,' said Adrienne.
'Why not?' asked Tyro, mildly. He had a gentle face and wrinkled clothes, no matter how new and expensive they were. But he was a genius, everyone said so these days, so it didn't matter as much as it otherwise would. Adrienne liked everything perfect. The whole apartment was white, white, white, and frequently photographed in smart magazines. Adrienne was an interior designer: very expensive, in every way.
'No, because I love you,' said Adrienne. 'And Christmas Day is so very special for us.' (It was, too. It was seven Christmas Eves ago that Cynthia had told Tyro she was pregnant again and Tyro, in panic and despair, had spent the next day with Adrienne and never come home; so Christmas was, as it were, the anniversary of their getting together, the dawn of their great love.)
'But if the children want to come –'
'No! Tyro, we have a child of our own now.'
And so they did. Tommy: three months old. The last six months had, for Adrienne, been perfectly dreadful, though Tommy had rather liked them. Adrienne had had no idea, or she'd never have got pregnant. She was just coming out of the nightmare.

'That doesn't mean the other three don't exist.' Tyro was being unusually obstinate. 'We could manage. I'd cook.'

'No,' said Adrienne. 'It's impossible. Bloody Nanny's got the weekend off.' It was their joke – Bloody Nanny like Bloody Mary – or rather Adrienne's joke. Neither Tyro nor Nanny thought it was all that funny.

When Tyro was out of the room, Adrienne picked up the phone and called Cynthia and said, 'Just you leave us alone. Stop whining and pestering. Live your own life, look after your own kids. They ought to be with you at Christmas anyway.' And she was going to go on about how Tyro was not going to pay Cynthia's telephone bill any more, it was time Cynthia tried standing on her own two feet, not sponging all the time, and her voice was beginning to rise and crack as it did when she was cross and sounding rather less like Fergie's and rather more like Janet Street-Porter's than she cared for it to be, when Tyro came back into the room, so she said instead, in her best lightly modulated voice, 'Cynthia, the children are all at school now, full time. Surely it's time you got a job? Then you could be more independent. You can't wallow in the past for ever. Tell you what, Tyro could take them all out for lunch on New Year's Day. I think he's free then. Wouldn't that be sort of symbolic and lovely?' Then, putting down the phone, she said to Tyro, 'How did you ever come to *marry* that woman? Were you depressed, or something?'

'We're giving a party New Year's Eve,' said Tyro. 'I won't be up to much on New Year's Day.'

'The children will hardly notice,' said Adrienne. 'Certainly not those three. They'll be too busy spreading the walls with tomato sauce. You'd think for the money we pay her your first wife would manage to bring them up halfway decently. What does she *do* all day?'

Adrienne was astonishingly lovely. Her lips were pink and clearly defined, her teeth little and white and even: so people tended to watch her mouth while she spoke, rather than listening to the words which came out. Perhaps that was part of her trouble: she'd never *learned*. And she was clever, and competent, and Tommy, even when Bloody Nanny took her bloody days off, lay quiet and good and beaming, perfectly tucked in, designer mobiles swinging about his crib just so. Perhaps Adrienne was just lucky, or perhaps if you deal with babies firmly and decisively that's how they are – who knows?

But now Adrienne saw Tyro standing there looking at her rather oddly, so she moved towards him and put her arms around him to put out of his head any wrong thoughts he might have and lured him into the bedroom, and pushed back the white-satin-layered-over-cream-suede coverlet on to the white carpet – and let him make love to her but afterwards he still said, 'All the same, if Cynthia wants Christmas Day off, and has somewhere to go –'
'No!' said Adrienne.
'Because if Cynthia found someone, and was happy, why then –'
'No!' said Adrienne, who found herself wanting Cynthia not to be happy even more than she wanted herself to be happy. 'No, no, no!'

Tommy would be properly brought up and would play in the nursery, as designed by Adrienne Charles – she was trying to patent it but it's oddly hard to patent nurseries – where there was everything a child could want and every surface could be wiped clean and there was a vacuum vent which you switched on over-night gently to extract dust and with the dust, germs, and there was a filter system which removed lead from the city air – and the fact of the matter was Adrienne did not want Tommy to think Alec, Alison and Edward were anything to do with him at all, just because they shared a father. Cynthia's children were plain, noisy and clingy: Alec whined, Alison sniffed, and Edward threw things. Sometimes she'd join them for a meal when Tyro took them out but only on Tyro's insistence. Edward would spend the time under the table, not at it, and nobody did anything to stop it and once when she tried to get up she found he'd tied the laces of her little cream eelskin shoes together. Everyone had laughed. She didn't let them come to the apartment. They'd hate it, just as much as she'd hate having them. At home they had Arsenal paper on their bedroom wall, or so Tyro said. How come Tyro *knew*? Adrienne wondered. He didn't surely *visit* Cynthia? No, of course not. The children must have told him: Arsenal wallpaper! She, Adrienne, felt and behaved as if her life started the day she met Tyro: why couldn't he do the same for her? Men and women were equal now: Cynthia had had the children more or less against Tyro's wishes, which made them hers, not Tyro's. Cynthia hadn't understood how Tyro needed space in which to work, to develop his talent. How could he do that, with three little children crawling round his feet? Cynthia had been selfish: had let herself go: got *fat*: couldn't help Tyro in his profession: had no friends in meaningful places: what had Cynthia *expected*? All their friends agreed. Most fathers just faded away after a divorce: she'd assumed Tyro would do the same. It wasn't even as if the children were charming or attractive. They were *horrid*.

So that was that. No! Tyro could take Cynthia's children out on New Year's Day when Adrienne would be busy cleaning up after the party. Bloody Nanny was taking Tommy home with her over the holiday weekend, which was a help. It was an important party.

Six days before Christmas Tyro went and brought home a Christmas tree, a real one, of a hopeless shape, and insisted on putting it up with Woolworth's decorations placed just anywhere, anyhow, instead of the elegant silver one she'd planned for the party: and the expensive crystal balls she'd just been and bought were altogether wasted. What was the *point*? She avoided making love with him for five full nights; she assumed he'd make the connection. And in the meantime she made lists and organized; all kinds of important and influential people were coming along. The green Christmas tree continued to look ludicrous in its setting, but she reckoned she'd persuade Tyro to take it down on Boxing Day. No one kept to the Twelfth Night ritual any more. They couldn't or the whole country would be awash with dead pine needles.

On Christmas morning, before they opened their presents, stacked all silver glitter at the end of the bed, Adrienne wrapped her long legs round Tyro's and forgave him, but he didn't seem to have his heart in it.

'What's the matter, my sweetheart, my darling, my genius, love of my love, light of my nights, my life?'

'Nothing,' he said. Well, of course he did. It never does to ask men what the matter is because they either refuse to say or don't know, or offer the wrong answer. So Adrienne sensibly just coaxed him back to happiness, and to focusing on her, which came to the same thing. She'd bought him a brilliant new suit for Christmas, for the party, made of a new washable silk which was meant to look crumpled even before it began. And he gave her a lapel brooch made of glass, diamonds and platinum, which was actually rather lovely but when she looked closer she could see it was made in the shape of a teddy bear, and who wore lapel brooches anyway? Men were always hopeless with presents. A teddy bear! They tried to turn you into a mother, and when you were a mother they got fed up and left. That's how her own father had been. She felt a surge of love for Tyro: the emotion made her helpless, and afraid, yet agreeably dependent, as if she were a child again. She put a little honey on a little square of toast and fed it to him: which was a real gesture since honey was so sticky, and it was only because Tyro insisted that she ever even had it in the house. But still he seemed somehow cut off. She hoped she hadn't overdone the no-sex run-up to Christmas: she'd made it all right now anyway. She loved him. He knew that.

He ate the proffered morsel – really he had no choice – but then he got up and dressed. He put yesterday's socks back on.
'I'm going now,' he said.
'Where?' she asked, startled.
'To see the children. I'm going to spend the morning with them.'

Afterwards she seemed to remember screaming: she hoped she remembered wrong: people should be civilized. But *Christmas Day, their* Christmas Day. How could he? But he did. Why? She couldn't understand. She must have been stunned, in shock. She wandered around the apartment alone and she wasn't wearing any clothes at all, and yet everything else was normal; just quiet and empty. She wanted to pick up Tommy but he wasn't even there: she hoped he was all right: of course he was all right. Bloody Nanny was trained to her eyeballs which was half the problem: Adrienne had had to give in over time off at Christmas for fear of losing her: at least she'd insisted the baby went with the stupid girl: a half-victory if not a whole one. Anger rose through shock: indignation: outrage.

She locked the front door against Tyro's return. She pushed his Christmas tree right over, she didn't know she was so strong: and there were needles everywhere and splintered bits of glass and she ground the awful crude chocolate nicknacks into the carpet – and then she picked up the phone to ring Cynthia but thank God, thank God, had the sense to put it down again. She started calling her friends instead: but they seemed cool, ever so cool.

Anthea said, 'So Tyro should see his children. It's Christmas,' and, 'I was going to call you. Philip and I won't be able to come on New Year's Eve –' and Philip was head of the Philharmonic PR.

And Dulcie said, 'Look, I'm busy. I haven't even got the turkey in the oven yet; you wanted Tyro, you got him, don't ask me to sympathize. And Sam and I can't come on Thursday night. Sorry and all that.' Sam owned the biggest chain of bathroom design shops in the country.

And David said, 'Darling, this isn't the time. I'm a bit busy,' and she knew what that meant and it upset her even more. She was used to David waiting and adoring in the wings.

And Maureen said, 'I don't want to hear anything more against poor bloody Cynthia. She isn't perfect but who is? Actually she and I are good friends nowadays, and Darryl and I came to a decision we somehow didn't come to when we should have and we're going to Cynthia's on New Year's Eve –' and Maureen practically ran Paramount, but that was nothing compared to the treachery.

And then there wasn't anyone else to ring; so she got through to Nanny who sounded surprised and said of course Tommy was fine, why shouldn't he be?

She rang her mother whom she hated and said Happy Christmas and hated her a little less. But her mother only seemed to care about Tommy, and made a fuss about him not being there, as Adrienne had known she would. Why had she even bothered? And where was Tyro, Tyro, her one true love: at least with three children in a poky flat he couldn't be *in bed* with Cynthia? Could he?

She rang Cynthia. The phone rang and rang. Perhaps he could. Perhaps Cynthia had dropped the children off somewhere – Adrienne was helpless: there was nothing she could do.

Adrienne wept till she was ugly. Adrienne put her teddy-bear brooch through the waste-disposal unit. Adrienne put Tyro's new silk suit through the heavy-soil white wash. Adrienne, by the time it was on the final rinse, thought, 'I've gone mad.' The thought calmed her down. It was madness to believe you could possess other people: re-create the world in your own interests. All the same, she tried Cynthia again. One of the children answered.

'Is that Alec, Alison or Edward?' she asked, quite nicely. 'Because this is Adrienne.'

'It's Edward,' said Edward. 'I don't want to speak to you. You're horrid.'

'Yes, I know,' said Adrienne. 'I'm sorry.'

'Oh well,' said Edward. 'Sometimes I'm horrid too. Everyone says so.' That made her laugh, and laughing, after so much crying, melted a block of ice in her heart, or that's how she described it to Tyro afterwards. Cynthia took the phone.

'I didn't ask him to come round here,' said Cynthia, before Adrienne could speak. 'In fact it's a bloody nuisance he's round here, because I've got a friend coming to dinner. Men always get their timing wrong. Still, the kids seem pleased. Mess everywhere. Why is it that the happier kids are the messier they are?'

'I really wouldn't know a thing like that,' said Adrienne.

'That figures,' said Cynthia. 'And what's the matter with you? You haven't said one nasty thing to me so far.'

'The Christmas spirit's got my tongue,' said Adrienne.

'Tyro's just leaving to get back to you,' said Cynthia. 'He wouldn't let me answer the phone the first time; he knew it would be you and he'd have to go. And this time Edward just picked it up before I could stop him.'

'Tell you what,' said Adrienne, 'if the children want to come back with him they can. If that helps you out, it's okay with me. It's a stupid sort of Christmas dinner with caviar and stuff, but there's lots of it. Only perhaps they want their turkey with you.'

'Well!' said Cynthia. 'Well, well! I've gone vegetarian so it's only mock turkey and lentils here; they won't mind missing that one bit. They're on their way.'

And so they were. By the time next Christmas came there was turkey for dinner, Tommy, under Adrienne's feet as if she were just any ordinary mother, played on a deep-rose carpet getting pine needles in his hair, and the nursery suite had been converted to bedrooms for when Alec, Alison and Edward came to stay.

'It's just so exhausting saying no,' said Adrienne, wearing the teddy-bear brooch Tyro had bought her to replace the one she'd somehow lost. Her new habit of saying yes brought its own problems, of course, but that's another story, for the summer holidays.

The Search for Mother Christmas

'Father Christmas and I,' said Ruby to her children, 'have a special relationship.' That was in 1971, when the boys were twelve, ten, seven and two respectively. Billy, Joshua, Jason and little Ben.

'Does that mean no presents this year?' asked Billy, who had a nervous disposition, and red hair like his father. Sometimes he was difficult to like.

'You mean a special relationship like between Britain and the US?' asked Joshua, who had been categorized as a gifted child. It had its drawbacks: he got called brainbox and was bullied in the playground.

'Does that mean he's going to be our new Daddy?' asked Jason, who lived in fear of some terrible event, which would come along and confound his life yet further.

And little Ben said nothing at all. He wasn't speaking yet. The clinic recommended he see a child development specialist and Ruby was putting it off. She had enough to do, as it was.

'It means,' said Ruby, 'Father Christmas may put the presents down the chimney on New Year's Eve rather than Christmas Eve because I don't get paid till the last Friday of every month.'

Ruby had a part-time job. She worked in the office of the local secondary school. The family lived in Garton, a small town in the new County of Avon, as unexciting as its name.

'There's no such thing as Father Christmas anyway,' said Billy.

'There is so,' said Joshua.

'Fancy you being ten and believing that,' said Billy.

Jason said, 'I know there's no Father Christmas because I waited up one night with a torch and it was Dad dressed up in a red gown with cotton wool.'

'What you saw,' said Ruby, briskly, 'was Father Christmas dressed up as Dad.'
And little Ben said nothing at all.

'Anyway,' said Ruby, 'he told me he'd come on New Year's Eve, and he wouldn't lie to me because I'm his wife.'
'Is that the special relationship?' asked Joshua.
'Yes,' said Ruby. 'I'm Mother Christmas and you can see I'm true.'
And she washed through eight socks and a pair of tights and draped them over the backs of chairs to dry by the morning. She couldn't afford to use the washing machine too often. She didn't own a dryer. In any case dryers shrink socks, ruin tights and help to deplete the ozone layer. There is some comfort to be gained from hardship, if you try, but not much.

Oh yes, that was the winter of 'seventy-one, when Ruby was thirty-four and two years widowed, and this was the pattern of her day:

Ben, waking at six, would wake his mother, and she would pot him, change him, dunk the drenched nappy, and give him a bottle to get on with (prepared the night before) and pack his bag for the nursery school where he had a free place. That put Ben on hold.

Ruby fed Pussy the cat to put an end to her yowling, and cleaned up after her. Pussy would not, would not, use the cat flap when it was cold. Ruby got the older boys' clothes laid out and mended and their socks sorted. If everything was in order it saved quarrels, argument and noise. (The three big boys shared a room. As they grew older it grew too small. Presently Ruby would have to move out of her bedroom and use a Put-U-Up in the living room, but she put that off too. Ruby was Canute sitting on a shore keeping back the tide that was her children.)

Then Ruby set the table and laid the breakfast. 'Sit down to breakfast, boys. Don't eat it standing up. Widows and orphans must make an effort.'

'Talk about it to them, Mrs Halter, talk about the accident. They'll get over it quicker.' All very fine, but what about me? Can't I just forget it? I have to peel my own mind raw for the children's sake? Apparently so.

'Well, boys, it was like this. Your father was killed reversing through red lights at the crossroads at two a.m. one morning. Walk round the corner and to this day you can see the dent in the lamp-post where his car ricocheted. Who was in the car with him? Why, Muriel his secretary. You know Muriel, she gave you knitted scarves for Christmas for years! Where are the scarves these days? They got the moth. Your mother threw them out. Yes, Muriel was killed too. Why was she in the car with your father? I expect they had some work to do together. Why two in the morning? It must have been very urgent. Very urgent. He'd rung me a couple of hours earlier and said he was in Edinburgh and described his hotel room to me. Can you get from Edinburgh to Bristol in two hours? I expect you can, if there are wings on your feet. No, dear, there isn't an air shuttle. I was speaking metaphorically. Then why did he, what was he, how was he – why was he reversing? Did he change his mind? What was there for him to change his mind about? Yes, I'm sure he said it was Edinburgh he was calling from. You wish to misremember but some things will not let themselves be misremembered. The fact of the matter is, my boys, my dears, some things will never be known, some questions never answered, and the more I think about it the more upset I get, and long for the Day of Judgement when the dead will rise up, when all will be made clear.

The truth of the matter being, lads, that whenever I got pregnant your father would find solace outside the marriage; and here I was pregnant with you, little Ben. Speak to me, Ben. What, speechless?

Once the child was born he would return; but of course this time, being dead, he could only send his ghost. If you are very good, sit up at the breakfast table, he may forgive you: not blow his cold breath through the broken windowpane. Billy, will you measure up and cut the glass? I will putty it in. We have no money to pay the glazier.

Yes, and I am sorry for the girls he took up with. Bit-part players in the drama of a marriage, thinking they were centre stage. Is that enough talk now, boys? Or would you prefer silence?

Never mind, never mind: the cereal running out and never enough milk: will four eggs make scrambled for five or shall mother go without again? And she missed him, she missed him: how could he go without her, taking someone else, not her? And where was his replacement? She saw no sign of him. How could he appear? She flew no flags saying, 'Here I am, take me!' There was no time, no energy, no money, to run one up the flagpole. Ruby's grey streaks stayed grey; Ruby got round quicker in low heels; how could Ruby buy nice clothes when the boys needed shoes? Ruby wouldn't go on the State, not she: Ruby wouldn't take handouts from anyone: Ruby would manage, yes she would. Oxfam helps the widows and orphans.

At seven thirty Ruby would wake the boys, remember whose turn it was to use the bathroom first, stop Joshua using the lawn, and if Jason had wet the bed strip it. Jason slept too soundly, the Clinic said. What's the answer? Pretend it isn't happening: poor little Jason, he's had a hard time. But so has Ruby, filling the washing machine and lucky to have it. Does no one care? Who's to care, now Jack is gone? A widow's an embarrassment. People cross the road. Misfortune might be catching. And wasn't there something odd about the death, wasn't he with some girl – never mind, never mind, what's the use of wasting emotion. I loved Jack and he loved me, most of the time, and we had children.

Seven forty-five. While the boys eat, make their beds so that when they get home from school all is orderly and cheerful, and a quick wipe round the sink, and a quick floor-sweep likewise. Then while the boys get their act together – Joshua has to have his books found for him every day – brilliant he may be, hopeless he is – and Ben and the cat have to be disentangled, and everyone got into coats and shoes which with any luck she remembered the night before to fill with newspaper and prop up against the Rayburn so they'd be dry, and Jason's cut his finger opening the cat food and needs a plaster – he always cuts his finger and there's an open tin unfinished and the cat's already been fed but never mind, never mind, if you shout at Jason he cries, and cries, and cries – and Billy puts an expression on his face which means he'd leave home yesterday if he could. Then distribute dinner money in the right change for everyone (it's every day now, not once a week. Someone broke into the school office one Monday and took the lot. Now it's collected daily, banked daily: people have to be so careful) and it's Billy's turn to clear the table but he's in a bad mood: better if she does it herself, she hasn't the energy to insist.

Eight fifteen and everyone leaves the house. Ten minutes at the bus stop. Off the bus to take Ben to the nursery (he's grizzling again. Ruby fears he hates the place: sometimes she's glad he can't talk. It stops him telling her) while Billy, Joshua and Jason continue on their own to school. They're too young. Ruby sometimes thinks of child molesters and child murderers, but not often and not for long. What can she do about it? Ben puts his arms around Ruby's neck and clings: he has to be dragged off: he wants to be at home with her, of course he does. And Ruby wants to be at home with him, of course she does. Or even without him.

Ruby wants her life back.

And it's still only eight forty-eight and Ruby's working day hasn't even begun: and Christmas is coming up.

'Ruby,' said her friend Margaret, 'why did you have four?'
'I wanted to get it right,' said Ruby. Ruby wanted a pregnancy in which Jack didn't fall in love with someone else. Ruby thought she'd got it made when she was eight and a half months' gone with Ben, until the news came about the crash, and her first thought had been if the car's a write-off how am I going to get to hospital? Ruby once told Margaret that Ben was an accident, but it wasn't true. The house just felt empty without a baby in it. Good God, why do women have such feelings: and worse, having them, why do they then act upon them?

As it happened, for the Christmas of 1971, Ruby's parents, though they disapproved of large families, helped her out. Father Christmas came down the chimney on the proper day. Ruby wanted the children to believe in Father Christmas. Ruby knew it was absurd: but it was her luxury, she needed it. And that Christmas Billy taught Ben to speak – only to say 'no', admittedly, but better than nothing. Perhaps. Was Billy disturbed by Jack's death? Not disturbed by his death at all but born to be like that anyway? How could one ever know? All Ruby could do was lay the table, light the fires, get them to school, make the beds so the place felt cheerful, keep everyone going, earn the money, work in a school so as to have school holidays, and dress up as Father Christmas once a year.

'How well you cope,' people said.
'What alternative do I have?' she'd ask. 'It's cope or die.'

Sometimes on a dark night she'd wish she'd had no children. Billy had been born when she was only twenty-two. She couldn't remember herself at all: Ruby without children. What had she been like?

And a decade passed, and the memory faded further and then the desire to remember failed. Ruby, widow, head of a one-parent family. It would do as a definition. It contained all necessary concepts of depression, hardship, loss.

When Billy was fifteen he started grabbing his brothers and getting their heads in headlocks and bashing their faces in.
'Better face it,' said Margaret, 'the boy's disturbed.'
'He'll grow out of it,' said Ruby.
Billy kept swearing at Ruby and saying she'd ruined his life.
'You have,' they told her at the Clinic. 'You let his father die.'
'What am I meant to do?' Ruby asked.
'Try asking his forgiveness,' they said.
Ruby did. 'Are you crazy?' shouted Billy. But she thought he was better after that. He just didn't choose to show it. Like his father, he had his pride.

Billy left school at sixteen. He hung about with friends and smoked dope and stopped beating up his brothers. He did a job here, a job there, and came back at odd hours with money in his pocket. What could she say to him? Get a proper job with a pension? Impossible to mouth the words. 'There is no future,' he'd say, if she tried to talk to him about it, and he'd cite nuclear winter or ecological disaster, but Ruby knew he meant the sudden full stop of his father's death, in the arms of the girl of his dreams, who was not his mother.

In the winter of 1981 Billy got a passport and said he was going to Australia. He had met a girl from Sydney called Liz.
'At least stay for Christmas,' pleaded Ruby. 'Bring Liz back as well.' And he said he would, but he didn't, and they cleared the two laid places and moved up the chairs and there was enough room for everyone. He sent a card from Sydney to say he and Liz were married.
'I expect she only married him to get British citizenship,' said Joshua. He was the one who had suffered most from the head-bashing. He was doing computer studies at a local college. 'She couldn't have wanted Billy.'
'Billy's so good-looking,' said Jason, 'anyone would want him. Not like me.' He had a Mohican haircut, and his head was shaved, but the school hadn't thrown him out.
'They can't throw him out,' Ben observed. 'If they did they'd lose Mum, and never has any woman worked so hard for so long for so little.'
Once Ben had started talking, he never stopped. Ruby wondered why she'd worried.

With Billy gone there was more space. She was astonished by how little she missed him. She was ashamed. One down and three to go. This was the pattern of Ruby's day once Billy had gone:

At six o'clock the dog woke Ruby barking to be let out, and she'd do it, and then let the cat in (her heart had hardened) and feed both and by the time she'd done that Ben would be out in the yard kicking his football against next door's fence – bang, bang, bang: of course they complained – and Ruby would say, 'Ben, not so early,' and he'd say, 'You said it was all right after eight o'clock,' and Ruby would say, 'It's only half past seven,' and he'd say, 'I must have dunked my watch in the bath again,' and Ruby would give up and lay the table and make the breakfast, and pick up yesterday's old pants and socks, and empty Joshua's ashtray (he said he liked the smell), and say 'Not so loud' to Jason's ghetto-blaster, and then Ben would come in saying he had frostbite and forget to close the door, and Ruby would ask Joshua to get in the coal and he'd say, 'In a minute', and she'd say, 'Now', and he'd say, 'When I've finished my scrambled egg. There isn't much of it,' and Ruby would say, 'That's because you didn't buy any eggs yesterday. None left for me. I can't really have to earn the eggs, buy the eggs, cook the eggs, clear up after the eggs all by myself, can I? And not even eat the eggs?' But the boys would not be listening. They would be reading newspapers, laughing at a story in *Today*, rolling over under the table with the dog (the dog had been for Billy; something to love: he'd never once taken it for a walk, never once), and their great boots were everywhere – and never mind, never mind, she loved them and they loved her, and now Billy was out of the way – callous, callous – it was at least cheerful. And then at eight fifteen they'd all leave the house (the beds unmade and the table uncleared: she got back first these days: she could do it then), and at least she'd learned to drive and had a little car, and a certain Mr Abbot took her out to dinner every now and then though Jason kicked up such a fuss it was hardly worth putting on a pair of earrings – and she was the official school secretary now and being sent on a middle-management course and she thought they might even take her on at the Education Authority –

That was winter 1981. That year Ben said, 'I wonder why Father Christmas always looks so much like mother?'
Jason said, 'How do you know he does?' and Ben said, 'Because I pinch myself to stay awake and I see from the light in the hall that Father Christmas is wearing a wig beneath the hood to make him look just like mother.' And Ruby said finally, 'Boys, there is no Father Christmas,' and they all just laughed and said yes there

is. And she wondered if they'd have dared, had Billy still been there.

And all of a sudden, for years creep on and over you so quickly, it was over. One by one the boys left home. There was space and peace and eggs for breakfast: even the animals calmed down: she could afford a new car: Mr Abbot could stay the night – she didn't want to marry him: she'd been married – the video stayed unbroken, the doorframes clean; she should have been lonely and upset and feeling useless, but she wasn't at all. She was herself again. She went to the hairdresser and finally had the grey turned into a rather expensive-looking hennaed brown. A Mr Roland vied now with Mr Abbot for her company. The three boys visited from time to time: they were all in London: they saw each other frequently. They had learned closeness: she was glad of that. She finally got her better job up at Education House. The cat died, poor old thing. She resolved not to have another, though she was tempted by kittens, of course. Who is not?

This was the pattern of Ruby's morning once the boys had left her:

She would wake in her own time (seven fifteen on the dot, true: some life rhythms, once acquired, take decades to break), put on a silk dressing gown and impractical slippers, make herself coffee and toast (scrambled egg on Saturday and Sunday) and go back to bed to eat, watching morning television, switching over at her pleasure with an unbroken remote control. After the eight o'clock news she would get up, wash and dress (flicking through a wardrobe – deciding) and, having more than one lipstick and eye pencils that were always sharp because they hadn't been used for telephone messages, make up her face to suit her mood. (Twice a week someone came to clean, change the sheets, empty the bins; oh, wonderful.) She would feed the tropical fish, inspect their quarters, talk to them. (Fish express their discontent quietly: of all pets they are the safest: they seldom pine: they are either well and happy or totally dead, floating belly-upwards, their erstwhile friends eating their innards.) At eight forty-five she would leave the house, calmly, and be at work at nine o'clock, to meet friends and colleagues with whom she got on well and for whom she had no moral responsibility.

Ruby rejoiced in her reward, so long in coming; this apparent happy ending.

But a manner of living, once yours, tends to be yours for ever. If the tide seems to stand still it is only illusion. It is on the turn, that's all. Back it comes. The crest of the wave becomes the trough, the trough the crest, in and in to shore. In the winter of 1988, three years into Ruby's quiet life, something happened.

Ruby received a letter from Social Services at Hounslow. Social Services said a young Australian – who named herself as Liz but would give no further information – had deposited small female twins at their offices, saying England should have them. The father, who according to Liz was English, had abandoned the family some years back: Liz did not see why his nation should get away with it. She did not want them: she had never wanted them. She named Ruby as grandmother, gave her address, and left. Could Hounslow Social Services make an appointment to see her? The girls, now in temporary care, were aged (they thought) perhaps five or six.
'No,' wrote Ruby, fervently and swiftly. 'No! Not on your nelly!'

They came anyway. None so determined as Social Services in search of a home for one stray child, let alone two. Ruby was their only hope. What did Ruby want for her grandchildren? Foster homes?
'Foster homes!' said Ruby. 'You've put your finger on it. That's exactly what I want.' And weakening just a little, 'Perhaps just one foster home. Twins! They wouldn't want to be separated.'
Social Services shrugged. Hard to organize. Ruby gritted her teeth (she was about to get them capped) and stood firm.
'Good lord,' Ruby said, 'who do you think I am? Some kind of all-purpose mothering agent? Besides,' she said cunningly, 'there

is no proof whatsoever these are my son's children,' and she sent Social Services packing, or thought she did.

Joshua, Jason and Ben were shocked. Of course they were. 'Callous,' they said. 'Mum, how can you. You just disowned poor Billy. This is your chance to make up for it.'
'The way your father died was enough to make anyone callous,' she said before she could stop herself.
They wanted to hear more but she wouldn't say more. She scarcely understood herself.
'Why won't you take your little grandchildren in,' they asked. 'They'd fill your life up. You must be so lonely. We worry about you.'
'My life is more than well enough filled up and I am not lonely.'
The boys wouldn't have it. 'Flesh is deeper than water,' they said. 'What you mean', said Ruby, 'is that blood is thicker than water, but I never understood what that meant and don't intend to start now.'

The boys claimed to feel relieved that she'd buried the dog when it died; not just dumped its poor old body in the bin. Callous! They'd never known their mother like this: capable of any cruelty, any irresponsibility.
'I can't possibly,' said Ruby. 'I'd have to give up my job. And supposing I failed with them the way I failed with your father, failed with Billy?'
'But you didn't.' They were astounded. 'Billy was just born like that.' She all but took offence. So she'd made no difference, had she? Wasted a life cooking, cleaning, rushing to catch the bus –
'You take them in', she said, 'if you feel so strongly about blood and water.' That shook them. They pleaded youth, college, freedom, domestic incompetence, of course they did. The last plea in the list was true enough. They couldn't even cook. Her fault. She should somehow have found time to let them make a mess of things: they told her so.

Ruby stretched her manicured toes languidly in the warmth of the central heating. 'Never, never, never,' she said. But Christmas was coming, wasn't it, the dangerous time of the year.

'Just for Christmas,' said Social Services, who knew they'd get her in the end. 'Poor little girls! They're pining for each other. Oh yes, separated now: one's in Lancashire, one's in Devon, and both now showing behavioural problems. Disturbed.'

'Headlocking? Bashing? Head-butting?'

'Good Lord no. We're talking little girls, not adolescent boys. Both too quiet and good for comfort.'

'One week,' said Ruby. 'One week, that's all.'

Judith and Jane, on the doorstep. They looked at her with Jack's eyes: two quiet good little girls with red hair like their father's. She felt spiteful towards them: she couldn't help it. Or were they Billy's eyes, not Jack's? Wasn't that even worse? Reproachful – why did you forget me? Aren't I your son, your flesh and blood as well? Why won't you grieve for me? See, I've left my children in my place, for you to do better. But this was stupid: they weren't Jack's eyes or Billy's eyes; they were just the eyes of any lost children who'd been taken here, left there, separated, joined, parted, not knowing why they were, who they were, in the end losing even the desire to know: children with shallow minds and empty hearts, without resonance: bright eyes growing duller year by year: causing work, work, work for whoever looked after them, and never a moment's peace.

Ruby slept badly on Christmas Eve. Children's noises woke her in the night. She was angry. She'd had enough of all that. She went into the living room, whence the noises came. Stop it, stop it, stop it! Her heart beat fast and furious.

Judith and Jane sat on the floor staring at the fireplace, waiting. Judith had a dustbin lid and carving fork; Jane had the frying-pan lid and the carving knife. Their little eyes were fierce and eager. They were together, intent, as one.

'What are you two doing out of bed? Go back at once!'

'We're waiting for this Father Christmas,' said Judith, unmoved.

'He's not allowed to come in,' said Jane firmly. 'This horrid person.'

'But he brings presents,' said Ruby. Did they know nothing?

'They're only pretend,' said Judith. 'He dresses up as other people. Uncle Jason said so.'

'No one asks him in, he just comes,' said Jane, 'all black with soot, Uncle Joshua said so.'

'We'll get him, we'll kill him,' said Judith.

'We won't let him in here. It's nice here,' said Jane. They both wore chainstore pyjamas, washed-out, faded, ironed into flatness. Brand-new mothers, same old story. Wash and wear.

'The nerve of it,' said Judith. 'Coming in where he's not wanted. When he should be at home with his wife. Uncle Ben said so.'

'Dirty old man,' said Jane, 'that's all he is.'

And they whetted their weapons on their tiny thighs, and gazed at the blank black chimney, their small midnight faces fervent, as they waited for the deceiver, the imposter, the divider of lives.

'This won't do,' said Ruby. 'Not at all. I have this special relationship with Father Christmas. He's my friend. I won't have him spoken of like this.'

And that was the end of Ruby. The little girls stayed, if only to learn better. One week became two, two weeks became months, months became years. And the terrible thing was, no one seemed in the least surprised, not Social Services, not Ben, not Jason, not Joshua, not even Billy, who actually one day sent a letter, to which Ruby replied, in affectionate terms, in pencil because she couldn't find a pen.

Ruby said to Margaret, 'Some women are born mothers, some women become mothers, and some have motherhood thrust upon them. I struggled against it all my life, but I think the truth is I was probably born to it. I don't do badly, I don't do well, I just do it.'

Merry Christmas, young and old, and may all your endings be as happy!

THREE TALES OF COUNTRY LIFE

A Move to the Country

Casey Green paced his living room and said, 'I can't go on like this.' He was six foot three and lanky with it, and his knees were somehow loosely hinged, and his living room was fourteen feet in one direction and ten in another, so his pacing seemed rather like that of a man in a prison cell, for all he was so comfortably at home.

'Can't go on like what, my dear?' asked Miranda Green, his wife. Miranda was five foot four and slightly built, and she could have paced quite comfortably, but didn't bother to. She perched on her stool at their breakfast bar, elegant – though scarcely long – legs crossed neatly at the ankles. It was 1974. Mini skirts were still half in and half out: Miranda kept hers two inches above the knee. She had good knees.

'Living in the city,' replied Casey Green, and the six adult yellow budgerigars in the big cage on the inner wall chorused their approval and the eight baby chicks tweeted to keep them company. It isn't everyone who can persuade budgies to be fertile, but Casey managed. Miranda didn't care for the somehow fusty smell that so many birds in a room create, but she liked Casey to be happy. 'Casey's my pet,' she'd say to friends. 'Casey's all the pet I need,' and so he seemed to be. Spiritually she combed and groomed him, and spiritually he preened. Casey and Miranda. They didn't have cats or dogs for fear of making the budgies nervous, though Hattie, their daughter, had recently come home from Hampstead Fair with a goldfish which they'd had to house. Goldfish are not happy in bowls, going round and round gazing at nothing: life in a prison: eternal boredom. Goldfish have to have tanks and water weeds and company: they need events, like anyone else: like all living creatures. Even an earthworm enjoys a challenge: an especially crusty piece of soil to penetrate: you can tell by the squirm of its tail. So Casey said. The goldfish had so far cost £43 to keep happy, and that was back in '74.

'I can't go on like this,' said Casey Green in May of '74. 'I can't go on living in the city.'
'Where else is there to live?' asked Miranda Green, in astonishment. It was 5 May to be precise. OPEC was getting its act together.
'In the country,' said her husband.
'Oh, Casey,' said Miranda, before she could stop herself. 'What a terrible idea!' Then she went off to her job as editor of a women's magazine. She wasn't very good at the job: rumour had it it was only hers because she'd had an affair with Astro Aster, the publishing tycoon. A totally unfair and untrue rumour, of course: but monogamy in those days was rare and a little unfashionable. All the same, the circulation of Miranda's magazine was dropping.

And Casey went off to his job as head of a design firm whose ideas were in worldwide demand, and got his secretary Wendy Dove to find him lists of country properties for sale.
'The country!' said Wendy Dove, who was five foot nine and what you might call strongly built, and wore trousers all through the era of mini skirts. 'What a lovely idea! If only I could afford not to live in the city! But what makes the country so nice is that there are no people in it, and the reason there are no people in it is because there are no jobs.'

Wendy was a clever girl, and Casey had once suggested to Miranda that she at least try Wendy out as a feature writer, but Miranda just laughed and said that was not the way things worked. Perhaps if Miranda had seen how they could or might work, the magazine's circulation would have risen, not fallen. Or perhaps it was merely that Miranda would not, would not have an astrology feature in her magazine at a time when all the others were going over to them – for everyone, it seems, likes to know what's going to happen next. (All Miranda kept saying, in her pretty clear voice, was this: 'Load of old nonsense. Won't have stars in my magazine.')

What happened next was that all of a sudden capitalism seemed at the end of its tether. OPEC put up oil prices: the price of petrol rose to 50p a gallon (no one could see how, if energy wasn't going to be cheap and freely available any more, cities could possibly continue), inflation went up another seven per cent, and on the day (11 June) that Miranda went to Harrods and found there were only two shades of tights available (light and dark) as if it were World War II again, it snowed. It was apparent that even the seasons were out of joint – a clear sign of impending catastrophe. That lunch time she went to a drinks party and was assured by a senior civil servant that ration books for food and necessities had already been printed and would be circulated by July, and in the afternoon she went to see Astro Aster, her boss, and was told it might be better if she went back to feature-writing and let someone else try their hand at being editor. 'Someone else' Miranda Casey imagined would be Teresa 'Tinkerbell' Wright, who had lately been seen at the Mirabelle with Astro Aster, but never mind all that: Tinkerbell was a good journalist and turned out to be a fine editor, and the magazine went from strength to strength, presently with two full pages in every issue devoted to astrology, and at least one or two surveys on the sexual habits and ambitions of its readers – always a circulation booster. No slouch, Tinkerbell!

'I think the end of the world is coming,' said Miranda to Casey that night. They drank champagne to cheer themselves up.
'The end of the city,' said Casey. Three budgerigars had been found with their feet turned up at the bottom of the cage. It had been a hot, hot June day and Hattie who was in the middle of her O-levels – once they were in July; in 1974 they were in June: if these days they are in May, why that's all the more time marking (which is paid) and all the less time studying (which is unpaid), so that can only be an improvement – had opened the windows and Casey was convinced the poor creatures had died of lead poisoning. Though some might say it was a nasty opposition of maleficent planets that caused this misfortune on this day along with so many others: not lead at all. Or perhaps Miranda was being punished for her lack of astrological faith. But how will we ever know?

Hattie came in from her History exam pale and crying and said she thought she'd failed every single O-level and she wasn't bright enough to get to University and all she'd ever wanted to do was work with horses, and why were her parents so horrible to her, and instead of saying, 'It's your hormones, dear,' Miranda said, 'We'd better move to the country.'

And so they did. Casey produced his estate agents' lists with a flourish. He thought they should go south-west – to Wiltshire, say, (horse country) or Somerset (goat country) – not too near London yet not impossibly far.

'Goat country?' asked Miranda, and Casey explained that Somerset was the kind of place where people bred goats to provide non-allergenic milk for babies. (The world was not yet additive- or colorant-conscious, but there were faint early ecological and nutritional stirrings down in Somerset, and Casey was conscious of them.)

'I don't think I've ever seen a goat close to,' said Miranda cautiously, and Hattie said, 'Well, I have and they're horrid; let's go to Wiltshire. Horses are groovy, goats aren't.' (The word 'groovy' was still just about passable, at the time. Just about. But Hattie never got things quite right.)

They found a house in Somerset, down on the levels, on the flat green peat plains; a property contained by the squared-off runnels of a network of dykes, edged with stocky, much-lopped willow trees. Five acres of it. They were in it within the year. They sold their London house for £40,000. (It is now worth £650,000. But it's no use thinking 'if only' in property matters. Though Casey was to, many times, like so many of us.)

'You'd have to have inner resources to live here,' said Miranda, nervously, the first time she saw the house. It was a square stone house with creepers growing over it, and a kind of flat blank look. Hattie shuffled amongst spring nettles in bare legs and shrieked, thinking a thousand insects were biting her, but she didn't move out of them. She'd never encountered such plants before. (She was a city child, and way back then school trips had scarcely been invented, so what was she to know about the country?)

'You have got inner resources, Miranda,' said Casey, firmly, and perhaps it was some kind of blessing, or else a command (after all, Miranda had promised to 'obey' Casey when she married him back in nineteen fifty-something, that being the habit of the times), because lo and behold all of a sudden Miranda did have inner resources. She put on her wellies and rubber gloves and unlocked the nettles from the soil, and remade the garden of Highwater House single-handed. She DIYed, and plastered and repaired one outhouse to make a design studio for Casey, and turned the old cider house into a study for herself. They meant to work and earn from Highwater House – he drawing, she writing. Casey would go up to his offices once a week: she would turn freelance, write articles about country life, visit editors and colleagues once a month. There was a post office, wasn't there, not so far away, and a telephone, and friends would visit: no need to be out of touch, not these days. How modern they felt – those days. (Though in retrospect, long, long before the days of the fax and the answer-phone and the bleeper and the cordless telephone and the high-speed train, it's hard to see how they could seem so. Perhaps the sheer amazement of reaching the moon back in 1969 – having rock-hard evidence that the skies were not magic but all too comprehensible – had not worn off.)

Wendy smiled and waited. She'd been brought up in the country. On Casey's days in town she made sure the office tea came in porcelain cups with saucers; she threw out the rough-hewn rural pottery mugs which were thick and rough on the tongue but all the rage. She said if ever he wanted to stay over he could: she had a spare room. Casey said no thank you.

Casey had an aviary built for the budgerigars at the bottom of the garden: it was architect-designed. (The locals looked on with amazement.) During the long hot summer the birds died of heat-stroke under the design-conscious glass roof. All but two, that is; a breeding pair fortunately; but something – badger, weasel, fox, who was to say – presently clambered in through the sluice tunnel and got those. Casey quite went off the idea of budgerigars. It was all too discouraging.

Hattie was right about her O-levels, at least. She failed the lot. Casey wanted her to go back to London and stay with aunts and go to a crammer's but Hattie wouldn't.

'You moved me here against my will,' she said. 'Now put up with the consequences.'

She took a job as an apiary assistant, tending bees for Peatalone Honey in hat, veil and long white handling gloves and gown. She looked bulky. She was never slim: heaven knew where she got it from – Casey thin to the point of angularity; Miranda with her hand-span waist –

Except within a short time Miranda's waist grew muscular and thicker. The calves of her legs grew broad and tough. Her chin was more determined: her eyes more shrewd. The third pair of rubber gloves (how quickly the brambles punctured them) were the last she ever wore. She lost interest in feature-writing, or perhaps it lost interest in her.

For the move to the country is not good, career-wise (the 'wises' came in that decade, and have never gone away, more's the pity), for journalist, musician or actor – anyone who works freelance and wants to be employed. You need to be in the heart of things – that is to say, not requiring the expense of a long-distance phone call to find you, nor likely to charge expenses for the journey up for an interview or briefing. If it's you or someone else a taxi-ride away, the someone else gets the job. But Miranda didn't mind. Miranda had her animals. Animals admire you, love you, need you, watch you: animals don't promote you and then demote you: animals don't prefer Tinkerbell Wright to you or judge you by the length of your skirt: they obey you, you don't obey them. The only thing is, animals multiply – then what do you do? Eat them?

'Eat them!' said Casey, of the twenty-four black-faced Jacob sheep. 'To the slaughterhouse with them, eat them!' They'd bought four in to keep the grass down. One ram, three ewes. That, in a season (for they were fecund and healthy sheep), made three rams, seven ewes. Two seasons on and the incestuous flock was up to twenty-four, and the young rams were killing each other, butting and horning to death, and there wasn't enough grazing land available.

'Eat them!' Hattie said. She was courting a fellow beekeeper, an eighteen-year-old lad with no small talk and red knuckly hands. ('She's not going to marry him or anything?' worried Casey. 'Of course not,' Miranda assured him. 'She's not as silly as that.')

No one wants to buy young rams; you can't even give them away. They got as far as the freezer and there they stayed.

'Let's not keep sheep any more,' said Casey. But Miranda didn't listen. She loved sheep. She bought a bigger freezer and gave joints away to the friends from London – though, unfortunately, they came visiting less and less often. They turned out to have been more colleagues than friends.

Then there were the dogs. You have to get a puppy if you live in the country. Of course the puppy grows up into a bitch and it seems unkind not to let nature take its course and before long you have nine more puppies and you can't find homes for all of them because the father's unknown (a puppy's father doesn't have to have a pedigree but it does seem to need an address) so you keep two –

And cats. Everyone loves cats. And hens. Chickens are adorable. Ducks are really witty. Geese are silly but brave. And all multiply.

'Why not stay the night?' asked Wendy of Casey. Wendy didn't even have a cat. She didn't like the smell of animals, she said. She could just about put up with a budgie, but that was all.

And dogs leap up and put muddy paws on clean clothes and these days Casey kept his good suits in the office and changed when he got there. He thought he'd better stay up in town a couple of days a week. The firm was busy.

'No thanks,' said Casey to Wendy, and he stayed with his aunts. But he did slap her bottom (no feminist she) and add, 'You're a very wicked woman, Wendy.'

Miranda was no longer interested in the rights of women, the vaginal orgasm, the cuisine of India or any of the things she used to know and care about. Now she read *Pigs and Their Care* and *The Happy Poultry Keeper* and Casey would crack open his breakfast egg (so many eggs!) and like as not find a baby chicken in it.

'I say, Miranda,' he said. 'Let's go on holiday. China, or somewhere.'
'I can't,' she said briefly. 'I can't leave the animals.'

'Stay over,' begged Wendy. 'You know you want to.'
'Can't,' said Casey, firmly. 'I love Miranda.'

Then Miranda got a goat. She got a nanny goat. Its name was Belinda. It was a delicate animal. Cold winds made it cough. It would be brought in to lie by the fire, in the evenings, with the four dogs. It smelt.
'Miranda –' said Casey.
'I know what you're going to say,' said Miranda. 'But the goat-house isn't wind-proof. I haven't got round to mending it yet. I've been doing the sandbags.'
Highwater House had not got its name for nothing. In a wet winter it tended to flood.

'I'm pregnant,' said Hattie. 'Since no one ever thinks about me I might as well get married.'
And so she did, to the young man with the knuckly hands.
She sank into the peat bogs without a trace except for three children in as many years: they lived in a council house and took *The Sun* and kept hens in the garden and were, or so Miranda thought, happy enough. Casey was horrified.
'Well,' said Wendy, 'you have to be careful with girls. Where they are is where they marry. Are you coming home?'
'No,' said Casey.

The nanny goat needed a billy goat. Miranda bought one in. It was very stubborn and Miranda's thighs were so black and blue from where she'd pulled and it had butted that she and Casey could seldom make love. One night the central heating failed and

Casey came home late from London – nearly midnight – and found Miranda asleep in a chair by the fire and the two goats lying on the marital bed.

'I'd move them', said Miranda, waking, 'if I could. But you know how stubborn goats are.'

'I'll soon move them,' said Casey, taking up the DIY axe.

'Don't be so brutish,' said Miranda. 'Besides, where else are they to go? I'm having heating put in the goat-house but it isn't ready yet.'

The next time Wendy asked, Casey said 'yes', and he never left her either. How sparkly clean Wendy's house was: it smelt of polish and scent: she sprayed her one pot-plant with insecticide. There was nothing living in the place except him, and her, and one well-trained busy Lizzie.

These days Miranda has a whole herd of goats, organically fed, and sells the best and finest low-fat goat's yoghurt to Holland & Barrett: she does a very good line in goat's cheese too. And the few friends who still call say to one another, 'But she's beginning to look like a goat – little mean eyes and stocky legs and a whiskery chin!' I'm afraid that they are right. But Miranda is perfectly happy about it, we mustn't forget that.

Chew You Up and Spit You Out

A CAUTIONARY TALE

'Well, yes,' said the house to the journalist, in the manner of interviewees everywhere, 'it is rather a triumph, after all I've been through!' The journalist, a young woman, couldn't quite make out the words for the stirring of the ivy on the chimney and the shirring of doves in the dovecote. She was not of the kind to be responsive to the talk of houses – and who would want to be who wished to sleep easy at night? – but she heard enough to feel there was some kind of story here. She'd come with a photographer from *House & Garden*: they were doing a feature on the past retold, on rescued houses, though to tell the truth she thought all such houses were boring as hell. Let the past look after the past was her motto. She was twenty-three and beautiful and lived in a Bauhaus flat with a composer boyfriend who paid the rent and preferred something new to something old any day.

'Let's just get it over with,' she said, 'earn our living and leg it back to town.'

But she stood over the photographer carefully enough, to make sure he didn't miss a mullioned window, thatched outhouse, Jacobean beam or Elizabethan chimney: the things that readers loved to stare at: she was conscientious enough. She meant to get on in the world. She tapped her designer boot on original flagstone and waited while he changed his film, and wondered why she felt uneasy, and what the strange muffled breathing in her ears could mean. That's how houses speak, halfway between a draught and a creak, when they've been brought back to life by the well-intentioned, rescued from decay and demolition. You hear it sometimes when you wake in the middle of the night in an old house, and think the place is haunted. But it's not, it's just the house itself speaking.

The journalist found Harriet Simley making coffee in the kitchen. The original built-in dresser had been stripped and polished, finished to the last detail, though only half the floor was tiled, and where it was not the ground was murky and wet. Harriet's hair fell mousy and flat around a sweet and earnest face.

'No coffee for me,' said the journalist. 'Caffeine's so bad for one! What a wonderful old oak beam!' The owners of old houses love to hear their beams praised.

'Twenty-three feet long,' said Harriet proudly. 'Probably the backbone of some beached man o' war. Fascinating, the interweaving of military history and our forest story! Of course, these days you can't get a properly seasoned oak beam over twelve feet anywhere in the country. You have to go to Normandy to find them, and it costs you an arm and a leg. And all our capital's gone. Still, it's worth it, isn't it! Bringing old houses back to life!' The girl nodded politely and wrote it all down, though she'd heard it a hundred times before, up and down the country; of cottages, farmhouses, manors, mansions, long houses: 'Costs you an arm and a leg. Still, it's worth it. Bringing old houses back to life!' Spoken by the half-dead, so far as she could see, but then she was of the Bauhaus, by her very nature.

'What's the matter with your hands?' the journalist asked, and wished she hadn't.

'Rheumatoid arthritis, I'm afraid,' Harriet said. She couldn't have been more than forty. 'It was five years before we got the central heating in. Every time we took up a floorboard there'd be some disaster underneath. Well, we got the damp out of the house in the end, but it seems to have got into my hands.' And she laughed as if it were funny, but the journalist knew it was not. She shuddered and looked at her own city-smooth red-tipped fingers. Harriet's knuckles stood out on her hands, as if she made a fist against the world, and a deformed fist at that.

'So dark and gloomy in here,' the journalist thought and made her excuses and went out again into the sun to look up at the house, but it didn't warm her: no, the shudder turned into almost a shiver, she didn't know why. The house spoke to her, but the breeze in the creepers which fronded the upstairs windows distorted the words. Or perhaps the Bauhaus had made her deaf.

'You should have seen me only thirty years ago!' said the house. 'What a ruin. I must have fallen asleep. I woke to find myself a shambles. Chimney through the roof, dry rot in the laundry extension, rabbits living in the walls along with the mice, death-watch beetle in the minstrels' gallery, the land drains blocked and water pushing up the kitchen tiles, and so overgrown with ivy I couldn't even be seen from the road. What woke me? Why, a young couple pushing open the front door – how it creaked; enough to wake the dead. They looked strong, young and healthy. They had a Volvo. They came from the city: they had dogs, cats and babies. They'll do, I thought; it's better if they come with their smalls: they'll see to the essentials first. My previous dwellers? They'd been old, so old, one family through generations: they left in their coffins: there was no strength in them; mine drained away. That's why I fell asleep, not even bothered to shrug off the ivy. I woke only in the nick of time. Well, I thought, can't let that happen again. So now I put out my charm and lure the young ones in, the new breed from the city, strong and resourceful. They fall in love with me; they give me all their money: but they have no stamina; I kept the first lot twelve years, then they had to go. Pity. But I tripped a small down the back stairs, to punish it for rattling the stained glass in its bedroom door, and it lay still for months, and the parents neglected me and cursed me so I got rid of them. But I found new dwellers soon enough, tougher, stronger, richer, who did for a time. Oh yes, I'm a success story! Now see, even the press takes an interest in my triumph! Journalists, photographers!' And the house preened itself in the late summer sun, in the glowing evening light.

'I say,' said the photographer to Julian Simley, as he wheelbarrowed a load of red roof-tiles from the yard to the cider house, 'you should get the ivy off the chimney; it'll break down the cement.' The photographer knew a thing or two – he'd just put in an offer for a house in the country himself. An old rectory: a lot to do to it, of course, but he was a dab hand at DIY, and with his new girlfriend working he could afford to spend a bit. A snip, a snip – and worth twice as much, three times, when he was through. Even the surveyor said so.

The house read his mind and sang, 'When *we're* through with *you*, when *we're* through with *you*: you can call yourself an owner, who are but a slave, you who come and go within our walls, for all old houses are the same and think alike,' and the photographer smiled admiringly up at the doves in the creeper, as they stirred and whirred, and only the journalist shivered and said, 'There's something wrong with my ears. I hear music in them, a creaky kind of music, I don't like it at all.'

'Wax', said the photographer absently, 'can sound like that.'

Julian Simley said, 'Christ, is that ivy back again? That's the last straw,' which is not what you're supposed to say when you're telling the press a success story of restoration, or renovation, in return for a hundred-pound fee, which you desperately need, for reclaimed old brick and groceries. 'I haven't the head for heights I had.'

'You fool, you fool,' snarled the house, overhearing. 'You pathetic weak-backed mortal. Let the ivy grow, will you? Turn me into weeds and landscape? Leave me a heap of rubble, would you! Wretched, poverty-stricken creature: grubbing around for money! You and your poor crippled wife, who'd rather fit a dresser handle than tile the kitchen floor! I've no more patience with you: I've finished with you!' and as Julian Simley stood on a windowsill to open a mullioned pane so the photographer could get the effect of glancing light he wanted, the sill crumbled and Julian fell and his back clicked and there was his disc slipped again, and he lay on the ground, and Harriet rang for the ambulance, and *House & Garden* waited with them. It was the least they could do.

'He should have replaced the sill,' thought the photographer, 'I would have done,' and the house hugged itself to itself in triumph.

'We can't manage any longer,' said Julian to Harriet, as he lay on the ground. 'It's no use, we'll have to sell, even at a loss.'

'It's not the money I mind about,' grieved Harriet. 'It's just I love this house so much.'

'Don't you think I do,' said Julian, and gritted his teeth against the stabs of pain which ran up his legs to his back. He thought

this time he'd done some extra-complicating damage. 'But I get
the feeling it's unrequited love.' The house sniggered.
'But how will we know the next people will carry on as we have?
They'll cover up the kitchen floor and not let it dry out properly,
I know they will.' Harriet wept. Julian groaned. The ambulance
came. The journalist and the photographer drove off.

'You want to know the secret?' the house shrieked after them. 'The
secret of my success? It's chew them up and spit them out!
One after the other! And I'll have you next,' it screamed at the
photographer, who looked back at the house as they circled
the drive, and thought, 'So beautiful! I'll withdraw the offer on
the rectory, and make a bid on this one. I reckon I'll get it cheap,
in the circumstances. That looked like a broken back, not a slipped
disc, to me,' and the house settled back cosily into its excellent,
well-drained, sheltered site – the original builders knew what they
were doing – and smiled to itself, and whispered to the doves who
stirred and whirred their wings in its creepers. 'Flesh and blood,
that's all. Flesh and blood withers and dies. But a house like me
can go on for ever, if it has its wits about it.'

The Day the World Came to Somerset

'You can tell the children by the mothers,' said Miss Walters. 'Show me a tidy mother; I'll show you a tidy child.' She spoke definitely. She always did. She knew what the world was like.
'Or the mothers by the children,' said Mrs Windsor, unexpectedly. But she was only an auxiliary; the staff room didn't take much notice of her. She was paid next to nothing. She came in from outside to hear reading, or help in the Infants Class, clearing up accidents or tying shoelaces. 'What I mean is, if I see a child who is happy and easy and bright, I know that child will have a kind mother.' But then, as Miss Jakes, who taught Class 4 and came from London, had remarked (in the new educational patois they all hated), Mrs Windsor was nothing if not child-centred. Soppy, that is.

East Bradley Junior was just about the smallest school in Somerset; threats of closure rumbled like thunder round its ears, and perhaps it was the noise of that thunder which deafened Mr Rossiter, the Headmaster, to the murmured protests of children and staff as he stalked the corridors, tall, grey, stooping, shouting and snapping at the children (and usually the wrong children), demanding peace, quiet and order in classrooms, school hall, staff room, everywhere; putting this out of bounds, declaring that out of order, putting pupils in corners for wearing red socks, disallowing trainers, and even standing infant wrongdoers in the wastepaper basket to prove just how worthless their chatter was. The two dinner ladies had caught his manner. Children who did not eat up were made to eat up, which kept Mrs Windsor busy cleaning up pupils who had been unexpectedly and distressingly sick. Mr Rossiter hated the PTA, but had to have one. The PTA raised money and the school was short of money. Without the parents, the school secretary would have had no typewriter, let alone paper for the endless notes, mess-ages and reproaches which streamed out of the school to the parental world. Mr Rossiter had liked the old days, when a line had been painted on the school playground and a notice above it said 'No Parents Beyond This Point'; even though the LEA's policy had obliged him to remove these in the mid-sixties, it was the mid-seventies before the parents had ventured over the non-existent line. But now there seemed no keeping them out. The new-style parents – mostly the ones down from London – would be in the classrooms before school, after school, chatting to teachers and pupils, even popping their heads round doors while lessons were in progress, with messages about aunties or swimsuits or lost packed lunches. Lots of pupils took packed lunches. Mr Rossiter didn't like that. It somehow loosened the school's grip upon the child. It smacked of change: change smacked of chaos.

The names on the school register changed, as the community outside changed. The ordinary Alans and Lindas and Michaels and Annes were sprinkled with Saffrons and Ishtars, Sebs and Felixes. The old stone villages were infilled with bungalows and housing estates: the farm cottages no longer housed farm workers – they'd been replaced long ago by tractors and the machinery of intensive farming – and who had to live on the spot any more? – but had been bought up by wealthy incomers from the cities, or let by farmers to hippy-style households – a safe enough thing to do, because the DHSS paid the rent – and in the meantime house prices went up, and up, and up – but who could blame the farmers? They had to survive somehow: no one wanted them to produce food any more. There was more than enough in the world, it seemed – all those people starved in undeveloped countries not for lack of food but because of someone else's duty to make a profit or be politically in the right. The waves washed right back to East Bradley's door, and changed the names on the school roll.

And the parents seemed to divide these days into the rich and the poor. New Volvos drove up to the school gates while from the school bus limped children who were wearing someone else's shoes, because the parents couldn't afford new; and the school fund was depleted paying the transport fares of children whose parents had to pay but wouldn't, and there were two small children who walked almost six miles every day on their own along an arterial road – little Ellen Bryce and Kelly Rice – and slept or wept all day in lessons. They were both from one-parent families: one mother out to work, the other in need of psychiatric help – or so Miss Jakes said. Miss Walters said Mrs Rice should pull herself together.

It was just about the prettiest school in Somerset: a low stone building next to a twelfth-century church, surrounded by fields: and there was an old oak in the playground, towering above the churchyard yews, which was reputed to be seven hundred years old. Ishtar and Seb, Saffron and Felix played tag around it, along with Alan and Linda, Michael and Anne, and little Cleopatra, too, black as night. When she was older the boys wouldn't go out with her, everyone knew. Though girls, later on, would vie to go out with her big brother Joseph. Okay, even stylish, for a girl to be seen with a black boy: all wrong for a boy to be seen with a black girl. Cleo got called names sometimes – nigger or black bitch – but Joseph didn't. But then Cleo was a tearful, meek little thing, and everyone liked Joseph, who was big, confident and good at football.

Miss Jakes talked about the problems of racism, which was seen in the staff room as absurd, and Miss Walters, whose brother was a police sergeant in Bristol, said the minorities had only themselves to blame, there was bound to be trouble: not quite 'why don't they go back to where they came from', but almost. There was an extraordinary occasion when a Mrs Havelock, a single parent who had come down from London and made a nuisance of herself on the PTA, and wore jeans and had fuzzy hair, demanded that Urdu be taught as a second language, as it was in Camden. Urdu, taught in London? Compulsory? The world was going mad. The world would have to be kept away from East Bradley, Mr Rossiter was the more determined, and the PTA must be allowed to talk, but not to act: let it confine itself to making money. Urdu!

Anyway, the day Mrs Windsor said you could tell the mothers by the children, the world came right up to East Bradley Junior School's door, and nothing was ever the same again. It came in the form of the Zambezi Boys: a band: a world-famous band, not quite rock, not quite reggae, all the way from Zimbabwe, once Rhodesia. A big yellow van, with 'Zambezi Boys' written on it, and some notes of music and a palm tree or two, stopped outside the school one Friday afternoon when the children were rehearsing their end-of-year concert. The driver, a small black man wearing dark shiny glasses, hopped out and asked Miss Jakes for directions. They were on their way to Taunton; they had taken a short cut: now they were lost. Miss Jakes pointed the way. The sound of Class 3's 'I am a Snowdrop' drifted through the open windows. Back got the driver into the van. The van would not start. Various members of the band – there were six of them, their leader a massive young man in a yellow gown even brighter than the van – got out, kicked it, or fiddled with the engine, or stood around discussing the matter – just like anyone else, as Miss Walters later remarked – and then asked to come in to call the AA. (Rebecca Ruddle, the AA man's daughter, was in 6A, and the only child in the school ever to have been in trouble with the police.) Which they did, from the school office. And then of course they had to wait for Rebecca Ruddle's dad. And the sensible place to wait was lined up against the back wall of the school hall while 2A sang, and the head boy, Harry Young, tentatively turned up the sound equipment – borrowed from Currys, whose daughter Melanie was in 3B – to make their tiny, timorous voices carry – and the children stopped paying attention to 2A's 'All Things Bright and Beautiful' and turned their heads to see these extraordinary, brilliantly gowned men (men in dresses) who all of a sudden were standing there. And then – no one quite knew how it happened, though afterwards someone said it was Mrs Windsor of all people who set it in motion – the Zambezi Boys were carrying their instruments in and setting them up, and giving a performance to the children and staff of East Bradley School. They, who could fill Wembley, not to mention Bristol's Colston Hall, they for whom the young of the world yearned and would empty their pockets (and other people's as well, no doubt, the way the world is now), played for the children of East Bradley School! And when the parents arrived, because when the time came to collect the children the Zambezi Boys were still playing, they got out of their Volvos and 2CVs and Austin Travellers, leaving them parked any old how, and peered through the windows, and the villagers did the same, because the beat was so loud and strong and extraordinary it had brought them all out of their houses. For Harry Young, usually bright and clean and tidy and responsible, got so carried away that he turned the sound system up, up, up, right up (and those drums and the synthesizer – or was it an African piano? – were loud, very loud, even by themselves). The crows rose and cawed for miles around, the heads of the sheep turned, and cows paused in their grazing, as the beat of Africa, so different from Somerset's slow, heavy heartbeat, escaped out of East Bradley School's hall. Look, Mr Rossiter was furious! But what could he do?

One (slow), two (slow), three-four-five (quick), the beat went, simple but not simple, somehow interlaced and interwoven. The children tapped their feet: the children shook their shoulders: the children looked at their teachers: their teachers were tapping too (but who could help it?) and then all were clapping, because the man in the yellow gown up on the platform was clapping his hands above his head – one, two, three-four-five – faster, faster, faster, now they were clapping on their own, and he was singing, what was it about? Sometimes in a strange language, sometimes in English, about brotherhood, freedom, jubilation, exultation – and Mrs Windsor was on her feet – dancing, Mrs Windsor! Which of the children was the first to move? Why, all agreed later it was little Kelly Rice who didn't have much to lose, who just didn't seem to care about Mr Rossiter – anyway, one of them was on her feet, jigging about, dancing, and then all the children followed, out of their seats, dancing, clapping, laughing – one, two, three-four-five – and the band roared its approval, and the great firm drumbeats and the laughing crash of the hi-hat got into the bloodstream, and Miss Walters (ever prudent) actually pushed chairs out of the way so no one hurt themselves, and took off her tight shoes to dance the better, and Miss Jakes just gave up and laughed and danced herself silly, and the parents stopped peering in at the windows and came in without so much as a by-your-leave and joined in, including Mrs – or what did she call herself? – Ms Havelock (even that seemed okay; let everyone do what they wanted: perhaps these singing, leaping men were speaking Urdu, in which case every word and not every tenth word they chanted or sang made sense), and Darren Gorren, the bus driver no one liked because he'd have no talking on his bus (not even whispering), came in and smiled and caught Miss Robinson of 4B by the hand and danced with her, and amongst the children friends danced with enemies, and enemies with friends, and the retired General Godden who put stones up on his patch of green to stop the parents clipping it with their tyres actually hopped about as best he could and his single strand of long white hair rose and fell to the beat; and look, on every fourth beat the man in the yellow gown leapt into the air, higher, higher, was it possible? He seemed held in the air, actually poised in the sheer energy of the music and the dance, somewhere near the ceiling, suspended by the animation and will of the Somerset children, old-style, new-style – up, up, stay-stay-stay – and as he stayed the church bell actually rang – dong, dong, just twice, on the beat – the vicar later said it must have been the vibration (thank you, Currys, for your technological assistance, thank you, Harry Young, for your act of grace, thank you, Zambezi Boys, for your wonderful performance) – and then Rebecca Ruddle's father the AA man finally turned up, and wondered what was going on, was everyone mad, and saw his daughter dancing and laughing and for some reason the shame of her disgrace was washed away (she'd broken into a Taunton pub with a group of older boys and stolen some cigarettes and had had to appear in the Juvenile Court), and he felt more cheerful than he had for months, and when he tried the Zambezi Boys' van the motor simply started – why it hadn't before he couldn't make out.

And as the engine started, the music stopped. The dancing, the cheering, the stamping died. And then little Ishtar Heddle flung herself against the door, arms outstretched. 'Don't go,' she cried. 'More! More!' 'More, more,' commanded the children, roaring and stamping – how could such little things make such a noise? – and the Zambezi Boys obeyed. The great obeyed the little. The beat began again, as if it had merely been waiting for the order: the guitar thrummed, the synthesizer sang, and down from the platform leapt the man in the yellow gown and grabbed poor flustered helpless Mr Rossiter by the hands and made him dance – made Mr Rossiter dance! – and dance he did, and as he danced his arthritis, or whatever it was that made his limbs so stiff, seemed to fall away, and Mr Rossiter smiled and stopped counting the children who wore trainers and planning his individual letters to parents – because didn't trainers make less noice than the clump, clump, clump-clump-clump of the properly black-booted children? – and he beamed at the staff, and he beamed at the children, and even at the parents, even at Ms Havelock, who was, even as she danced, quite startled. Then, as suddenly as it began, it stopped.

'Peace, exultation, jubilation', cried the young man in the yellow gown who could be sustained in mid-air by the energy of his being, 'to the brotherhood of man!'
'And the sisterhood!' cried Ms Havelock. 'Don't forget the sisterhood.' And they were gone. The Zambezi Boys were gone.

And after that nothing was quite the same, if only that Scott Hockney in Infants never dirtied his pants again – perhaps a miracle, or just because he'd jigged about so much he got some kind of control over his muscles – so the other children would play with him (and Mrs Windsor reported he could remember that the mysterious t-h-e spelt the extraordinary 'the' from the next Monday right through to the next Friday and for ever thereafter). And Ms Havelock took to going miles out of her way each day to take and fetch Kelly and Ellen in her 2CV instead of saying that to do so was system-bolstering and a child or two would have to die before the under-three-mile-no-free-transport system was reformed. And Neal Hodder's Dad, who'd also danced, decided on the whole he'd better not crop-spray the field behind the school in spite of the stuff's being officially specified safe; and everyone wore trainers ever after, they being so much better for dancing, and no one kept their Kit-Kats and crisps to themselves at break, as had lately been their habit (for the greed and self-interest of governments is as catching as measles), but began to share them with the limping children off the bus, who no longer limped because trainers can be cheap and interchangeable – was not this the brotherhood, not to mention the sisterhood, of man, not to mention woman? And the dinner ladies cooked a little better and with more charity, so the children ate up better; and at the first sign of trouble there'd be a kind of thrumming of fingers on desks – one, two, three-four-five – and the trouble evaporated; and if Mr

Rossiter felt his anxiety and irritation returning, and began to express it, there'd be a kind of dancing note thrumming on the floor as the children fell into step – one, two, three-four-five – on the stairs and down the corridors, and he'd hold his tongue, and just nod, and smile, and not a word had to be said; and little Cleo put her hand in Miss Walters', who let it stay there, and even put her up for the Class Achievement Award, and the wastepaper basket in the Infants somehow got lost and was never found again. One, two, three-four-five.

Nothing was ever the same again after the Zambezi Boys came to East Bradley by mistake, on their way to Taunton, and brought with them in their yellow van the good things of the wider world – exultation, jubilation, joy, the throb of the universe – and in their easy generosity passed them on. Such things happen. That was the day the world came to Somerset, and couldn't be kept out.

AS TOLD TO MISS JACOBS

A Gentle Tonic Effect

'What did you say your name was?' asked Morna Casey. 'Miss Jacobs? Just a miss? Not a doctor or anything? Well, *chacun à son goût*. But tell me, do you need planning permission, or can anyone just set up in their front room and start in the shrinking business?'

Morna Casey frowned at what she thought might be a hangnail, and looked at her little gold watch with the link chain, and waited for Miss Jacobs' reply, which did not come.
'I have very little time for people who go to therapists,' added Morna Casey. 'I'm sorry, but there it is. It's so sort of self-absorbed, don't you think? I can't stand people who make a fuss about nothing. If it wasn't that my dreams were interfering with my work I wouldn't be here.'

Still no response came from Miss Jacobs: she did not even lift her pencil from the little round mahogany table at her side.

'You charge quite a lot', observed Morna Casey, 'for someone who says so little and takes no notes. But if you can get away with it, good for you. I suppose on the whole people are just mentally lazy: they employ analysts to think about them rather than do it themselves.'

Morna Casey waited. Presently Miss Jacobs spoke. She said, 'This first consultation is free. Then we will see whether it is worth both our whiles embarking on a course of treatment.'

'I don't know why,' said Morna Casey, 'but you remind me of the owl in *Squirrel Nutkin*.'

A slight smile glimmered over Miss Jacobs' lips. Morna Casey noticed, of course she did. She had declined to lie down on the leather couch, with her head at Miss Jacobs' end, as patients were expected to do.

'I suppose', acknowledged Morna Casey, 'it's because I feel like Squirrel Nutkin, dancing up and down in front of wise old owl, making jokes and being rude. But you won't get to gobble me up: I'm too quick and fast for the likes of you.'

Morna Casey was a willowy blonde in her late thirties: elegantly turned out, executive style. Her eyes were wide and sexy, and her teeth white, even and capped. She wore a lot of gold jewellery of the kind you can buy in Duty Free shops at major airports. Her skirt was short and her legs were long and her heels were high.

'I went to see a doctor,' said Morna Casey, 'which is a thing I hardly ever do – I can't stand all that poking and fussing about. But the nightmares kept waking me up; and if you're going to do a good job of work it's imperative to have a good night's sleep. I've always insisted on my beauty sleep – when Rider was a baby I used ear plugs: he soon learned to sleep through.'

Rider was Morna Casey's son. He was seventeen and active in the school potholing club.

Morna Casey leaned forward so that her shapely bosom glowed pink beneath her thin white tailored shirt. She wore the kind of bra which lets the nipples show through.
'The fool of a doctor gave me sleeping pills, and though I quadrupled the dose it still didn't stop me waking up screaming once or twice a night. And Hector wasn't much help. But then he never is.'

Hector was Morna Casey's husband. He was head of market research at the advertising agency where Morna worked. She was a PR executive for Maltman Ltd, a firm which originally sold whisky but had lately diversified into pharmaceuticals.

'Helping simply isn't Hector's forte,' said Morna Casey. 'You ask what is? A word too crude for your ears, Miss Jacobs, probably beyond your understanding; that's what Hector's forte is. I first set eyes on Hector in a pub one night, eighteen years ago: I said to my then husband, "Who's that man with the big nose?" and Hector followed us home that night and we haven't been apart since.'

Miss Jacobs looked quite startled, or perhaps Morna Casey thought she did.

'People say "Didn't your husband mind?" and I reply, "Well, he didn't like it much but what could he do?"' said Morna Casey. 'He moved out, which suited me and Hector very well. It was a nice house: we bought him out. Hector's one of the most boring people I know: he has no conversation apart from statistics and a very limited mind, but he suits me okay. And I suit him: he doesn't understand a word I say. When I tell him about the dreams, all he says is, "Well, what's so terrible about dreaming that?" It was the doctor who suggested I came to see you: doctors do that, don't they? If they're stumped they say it's stress. Well, of course I'm stressed: I've always been stressed: I have a difficult and demanding job. But I haven't always had the dreams. I told the doctor I was perfectly capable of analysing myself thank you very much and he said he didn't doubt it but a therapist might save me some time, and time was money, which is true enough, and that's the reason I'm here. At least all you do is poke about in my head and not between my legs.'

Miss Jacobs took up her notepad and wrote something in it.

'What's that?' asked Morna Casey, nastily. 'Your shopping list for tonight's dinner? Liver? Brussels sprouts?'

'If you'd lie down on the couch,' said Miss Jacobs, 'you wouldn't see me writing and it wouldn't bother you.'

'It doesn't bother me,' said Morna Casey. 'Sorry. Nothing you do bothers me one little bit, one way or another. And nothing will make me lie down on your couch. Reminds me of my father. My father was a doctor. He smoked eighty cigarettes a day and died of lung cancer when he was forty-three and I was seventeen. He'd cough and spit and gasp and light another cigarette. Then he'd inhale and cough some more. I remember saying to my Uncle Desmond – he was a doctor too – "Do you think it's sensible for Daddy to smoke so much?" and Uncle Desmond replied, "Nothing wrong with tobacco: it acts as a mild disinfectant, and has a gentle tonic effect." I tend to believe that, in spite of all that research – paid for by the confectionery companies, I wouldn't be surprised – about the tobacco–lung-cancer link. It's never been properly proved. The public is easily panicked, as those of us in PR know. My father enjoyed smoking. He went out in his prime. He wouldn't have wanted to be old.

'But I'm not here to waste time talking about my father. When you're dead you're dead and there's no point discussing you. I'm here to talk about my dream. It comes in two halves: in the first half Rider is miniaturized – about twenty inches long – and he's clinging on by his fingertips to the inside of the toilet, and crying, so I lean on the handle and flush him away. I can't bear to see men crying – and at seventeen you're a man, aren't you. That part of the dream just makes me uneasy; but then out of the toilet rise up all these kind of deformed people – with no arms or two heads or their nerves outside their skin not inside so they have a kind of flayed look – and they sort of loom over me and that's the bit I don't like: that's when I wake up screaming.'

Morna Casey was silent for a little. She stretched her leg and admired her ankle.

'I think I understand the first part of the dream,' said Morna Casey presently. 'I gave birth to Rider in the toilet bowl at home. I wouldn't go to hospital. I wasn't going to have all those strangers staring up between my legs, so when I went into labour I didn't tell a soul, just gritted my teeth and got on with it, and it ended up with Hector having to fish the baby out of the water. Now Rider climbs about in potholes – he actually likes being spreadeagled flat against slimy rock faces, holding on with his fingertips. His best friend was killed last year in a fall but I don't worry. I've never worried about Rider. What's the point? When your number's up your number's up. Sometimes I do get to worry about the way I don't worry. I don't seem to be quite like other people in this respect. Not that I'd want to be. I guess I'm just not the maternal type. But Rider grew up perfectly okay: he was never much of a bother. He's going to university. If he wants to go potholing that's his affair. Do we stop for coffee and biscuits? No? Not that I'd take the biscuits but I like to be offered. Food is an essential part of PR. The laws of hospitality are very strong. No one likes to bite the hand that feeds them. That's one of the first things you learn in my job. You should really seriously think about it, Miss Jacobs.'

Morna Casey pondered for a while. A fly buzzed round her head but thought better of it and flew off.

'I don't understand the second part of the dream at all,' said Morna Casey presently. 'Who are all these deformed idiots who come shrieking out of the toilet bowl at me? I really hate the handicapped. So do most people only they haven't the guts to say so. If there'd been one single thing wrong with Rider, an ear out of place, oesophagus missing, the smallest thing, I'd have pushed him under, not let Hector fish him out. Don't you like Rider as a name? The rider of storms, the rider of seas? No one knows how poetic I am: they look as I go by and whistle and say, there goes a good-looking blonde of the smart kind not the silly kind, and they have no idea at all what I'm really about. I like that. One day I'm going to give it all up and be a poet. When Hector's old and past it I'm going to push him under a bus. I can't abide dribbly old men. When I'm old Rider will look after me. He loves me. He only clambers about underground to make me notice him. What he wants me to say is what I've never said: "I worry about you, Rider." But I don't. How can I say it; it isn't true.'

Miss Jacobs raised an eyebrow. Morna Casey looked at her watch.

'I have a meeting at three thirty,' said Morna Casey. 'I mustn't let this overrun. I'm on a rather important special project at the moment, you may be interested to know. I'm handling the press over the Artefax scare.'

Artefax was a new vitamin-derivative drug hailed as a wonder cure for addictions of all kinds, manufactured by Maltman and considered by some to be responsible for a recent spate of monstrous births – though Maltman's lawyers had argued successfully in the courts that, as the outbreaks were clustered, the Chernobyl fallout must be to blame – particles of caesium entering the water table in certain areas and not in others.

'So you'll understand it's all go at the moment,' said Morna Casey. 'We have to restore public confidence. Artefax is wonderful, and absolutely harmless – you can even take it safely through pregnancy; you're not addicted to anything, and all it does is have a mild tonic effect. Our main PR drive is through the doctors.'

Morna Casey was silent for a little. Miss Jacobs stared out of the window.

'Well yes,' said Morna Casey presently. 'I see. If I changed my job the dreams would stop. But if I changed my job I wouldn't worry about the dreams because it wouldn't matter about the job, would it. All the same I might consider a shift in career direction. I don't really like working for the same outfit as Hector. It does rather cramp my style – not that he can do much about it. I do as I like. He knows how boring he is; what can he expect?'

'There's a good opening coming up,' said Morna Casey, 'or so I've heard on the grapevine, as head of PR at Britnuc; that's the new nuclear energy firm. I think I'd feel quite at home with radioactivity: it's like nicotine and Artefax – in reasonable quantities it has this gentle tonic effect. Of course in large quantities I daresay it's different. But so's anything. Like aspirin. One does you good, two cure your headache, twenty kill you. In the Soviet Union the spas offer radioactive mud baths. Radon-rich, they say. They're very popular.'

'Thank you for the consultation, Dr – sorry, Miss – Jacobs. I won't be needing to see you again. I'm much obliged to you for your time and patience: though of course one can always do this kind of thing for oneself. If I ever give up PR I might consider setting up as a therapist. No planning permission required! A truly jolly *pièce de* rich *gâteau*, if you ask me.'

And Morna Casey adjusted her short taupe skirt over her narrow hips and walked out, legs long on high heels, and Miss Jacobs, whose hand had been hovering over her appointment book, put down her pencil.

Moon Over Minneapolis or
Why
She
Couldn't
Stay

Miss Jacobs, you thought I was safely off your hands. You thought I would never return to lie like an idiot with my feet towards your window, my head towards your chair, at fifty pounds an hour, and think myself lucky. Have you changed the couch since I last lay here? I'll swear it's harder. It used to feel like an operating table on which I lay stretched while an operation was performed upon my brain without anaesthetic. But there was at least some padding beneath me. Now it's more like a coffin: I lie on bare planks, unseasoned, roughly nailed together, as I suppose the coffins of the homeless, of criminals, of derelicts, to be. Those who have nobody. I am a corpse, a talking corpse. Is that what you had in mind for your patients, Miss Jacobs? What you meant when you changed the couch (not before time, I may say: the drumming heels of the desperate, the dying, had quite worn the green velveteen down the far end)? To move us yet further out of comfort into discomfort? Like one of those mean and judgemental parents who say to the child, 'You've got to learn what the world is like – start now!'

No, before you say anything, my parents were neither mean nor judgemental: on the contrary, they veered towards the over-generous and the careless. They could give nothing its proper attention. They were too busy.

A corpse which talks. Very well, I accept my own definition. That is what it feels like. The mouth continues for a time after death to open and shut, open and shut, and a thin stream of words flows out like liquid forced up by convulsing lungs. When even that fails, I will finally be quiet.

No, I did not kill myself. What happened was that my sister finally killed me. I always knew she would. She made me come home from Minneapolis. She didn't have to fire a gun into the wedding marquee, or spike my champagne with cyanide; she didn't have to utter a word of reproach; all she had to do was exist. I don't blame her. I just hate her.

I cross my hands on my chest as if I were the corpse she made me. My breasts stick up too high for comfort and convenience. She always envied me my breasts. They are too large for corpsely grace, for true refinement. But she won't accept that: she would rather envy me. Envy is her stock in trade. When we were thirteen we measured ourselves and compared notes. My chest was definitely half an inch larger than hers, yet we were supposed to be identical in every way. Minnie took it as yet another sign of my privilege, the unfair blessing which fate kept heaping upon my poor bowed shoulders. Personally, I longed to be flat-chested, then as now. Clothes hang better. But try telling Minnie that.

Minnie my murderer. Miss Jacobs, I swear I did not know that Tom came from Minneapolis. The Midwest, he said. A city of lakes, of spires, of flour mills old and new, of grace and contemporary art; well, sixties art – a Rauchenberg, a Lichtenstein or so in the Walker, a splatter-burst of mess contained in the cleanest white shapes available to the architectural imagination.

What, you haven't been to the Walker, Miss Jacobs? Of course you haven't. You have sat here in this room for ever, you will be here for ever: you are the dustbin into which we scrape all our left-overs; we, me and my siblings, your other clients. The ones you so carefully don't let me see. Come in this door, go out that! Once I stood in the shadows of the trees on the other side of the road for a whole Tuesday and watched your back door. They came out at hourly intervals but there was no one amongst them I knew, or anyone who was of any interest to me. Such a dull collection of others, denatured because they had left so much of themselves with you, the analyst. You are going out of fashion, I hope you know that? Freud is debunked – a Viennese neurotic: Klein neglected – what is this good breast bad breast junk? Adler exposed – family order, tests tell us, has no effect whatsoever upon personality. Only Jung is in fashion, with his yin and yang, his animus and anima, all that dreamy let's-love-one-another touchy-feely stuff. Are you listening to me? Are you asleep? Or are you knitting again? Click, click, click! You told me you were taking notes, that was what the sound was, but I think you were lying. Knitting needles click; pens don't. Or perhaps you're chewing gum and your dentures are loose? I would push myself up and turn my head and look but I daren't: I might see the devil's face, I might see you weren't there at all, just a black cat sitting in your chair, the Dark Thing, and anyway I can't move, I'm dead. Minnie killed me. I can see my clasped hands in front of me. White dead hands. Tom loved my hands. The polish on my right little fingernail is chipped. Fancy lying in a coffin with a chipped nail. I thought they were supposed to see to that sort of thing.

Yes. I believe there is always a They about to clean up and explain, even as they persecute. Silly old me.

I know you believe I chose Tom because he came from Minneapolis, in order to upset Minnie more. But I didn't choose. He just happened along. A millionaire from the Midwest, a transatlantic knight in shining armour to pluck me out of the muddy swamp, detect my beauty through my tangled hair and carry me off to happiness and prosperity. His City of Exit didn't seem too important to me. Look, there aren't so many knights in shining armour around. Had one come along from Milwaukee, I'd have gone for him. Honest.

Minnie was a stupid name anyway. Neither of us liked it. They called me Rosamund because that was the name Frank and Tillie had chosen for their first-born. Frank and Tillie are my parents. What was that you murmured? Christ, she actually spoke. Miss Jacobs, who gets a pound a minute, actually spoke! 'I haven't forgotten.' That's what you say. How am I supposed to know when you're listening or when you're asleep? Whether you've absorbed everything, or nothing? Whether you've forgotten what once you knew, or whether you never knew to begin with? The permutations of your not knowing are endless. And it has been a year since I was last here. More time than you'd need to forget.

Nothing is making me angry. What makes you think I'm angry? I'm upset, that's all, lying here again, having to push and shove amongst your other patients, waiting for a cancellation. What do you think that feels like? Do you understand my humiliation? I thought I could cope and I can't. I'm unhappy. I loved Tom. Where am I ever going to find another man like him again? He'll never speak to me again. Everything was organized: a wedding ceremony in a chapel of love with the kind of service Americans love: bits and pieces of poetry and flute solos, and his parents, and his grandparents, and his friends and their friends and apple pie; and I couldn't, I couldn't. I said I wouldn't. It was the moon. Oh Christ. Can I go to the loo? I suppose I'm allowed?

Where was I? Oh yes, Minnie being Minnie and me Rosamund. How could Frank and Tillie have done it to her? To me? Something else for her to moan about. The first and final straw. Minnie the afterthought. Well, she was, wasn't she? Out she popped after me, completely unexpected, two pounds lighter, two inches shorter, for all we were meant to be identical. People in the States seem to think there are degrees of identical: but how can that be? Monozygotic is what it says. One cell split. Same genes exactly. Except it isn't like that, is it? I reckon between us Minnie and I have a hundred per cent of various qualities and we share them out, not necessarily evenly. Niceness, for example. I have seventy per cent. Minnie has thirty per cent. Envy. I have twenty per cent. Minnie got the eighty per cent. Minnie's envy has killed me.

Other children spend their lives saying, 'It isn't fair. It isn't fair.' I have to spend mine saying, 'I can't help it.' I can't help being prettier than her (I reckon that's another kind of quality, nothing to do with actual looks: a lot to do with self-image: I had sixty per cent, she had forty per cent), cleverer than her, fifty-five: forty-five (but enough to get me to college, her not), luckier than her (well, look at her children!), funnier than her (eighty: twenty), more sociable than her (sixty-five: thirty-five). The friends came to see me: she tagged along, sulking. But I loved her, Miss Jacobs. That made it worse. She knew I loved her, and she couldn't even do that: love me back. She resented me too much. Capacity for love: Rosamund ninety per cent, Minnie ten per cent. She made my life miserable. If I passed an exam, fell in love, had a baby, bought a house, I couldn't rejoice. All I could think was, oh my God, will it upset Minnie? How can I hide it?

When Peter and I discovered our first house had dry rot and it was going to cost thousands to repair, the first thing I thought was, thank God, that'll make Minnie feel better. When Peter was killed in his car accident I remember thinking, at least now I'm a widow, that's something. But all she said was, 'My, you do look good in black. Is that why you're wearing it?'

Going over old ground? You actually remember the ground we trod? Good Lord! I left suddenly, didn't I? I didn't think you'd notice. You sent me a massive bill and a kind of note. It registered pathetic, the way notes from former lovers do; all the energy drained away. What was once important no longer is. You ought to come back, you said; you left too soon. Finish your treatment. It sounded like Minnie-talk to me. The reproach there, even if others don't hear it. Ought, ought, ought: never enjoy, love, live! Minnie, murderer of my life. Sharer of my womb. I never complain that she took my nourishment from me: she's always going on about how greedy I was, pushing past her at the post. They said I was lying further back than her: by rights I was the one who should have been born second. She would have been first, would have been given 'Rosamund', the great prize: I would have been Minnie. And I'd still have been me, and now would be living in Minneapolis. Minnie of Minneapolis. Why in God's name didn't she have the guts to elbow me out of the way? Because she's so feeble, that's why.

Minneapolis is a twin city. Did you know that? I didn't, till we were on this aircraft and the captain said, 'Fifty thousand feet and on our way to the twin cities of Minneapolis and St Paul,' and I said to Tom, 'What does he mean, what does he mean?' We were flying First Class. Have you ever flown First Class? I shouldn't suppose so. It's so comfortable. You feel better than anyone else in the world. I was surprised Minnie hadn't somehow got herself on to the flight, Economy Class, of course, pushing her head through the curtains with the snarl she uses for a smile, saying, 'Hi, Rossie.' She'd never call me Rosamund. Since she didn't have a Minnimund equivalent, she wouldn't. Whenever I really wanted to wind her up I'd call her Minnimund. And Frank and Tillie would be there in Club Class looking uneasy and doing nothing to stop her except saying, 'We love you too, Minnie; you're very dear to us. All the dearer because you were unexpected.' Lies, lies. Rearing twins is hell. They never had any more children after us: they couldn't face it. I reckon Minnie, by being born, deprived another two or three putative children of life, I really do.

Anyway Tom said, 'Why, they're twin cities. The Mississippi divides them. They're rivals. Minneapolis is the modern, go-getting, thrusting city. St Paul is the older, ramshackle one. It kind of limps along behind, but always feels superior.'
'But that means,' I said, 'they're only half a city each.' He pretended not to hear. Anything he didn't understand he pretended not to hear. It was his one big fault. I could have lived with it.

St Paul, limping along behind. Minnie's first child, Andrew, was born with a dislocated hip and her husband Horace didn't believe in doctors so he grew up dragging a leg behind him. And Lois, Minnie's little girl, wasn't the greatest beauty ever born, and Minnie made it worse by calling her Uglymug and saying, 'Just my luck!' As if it was her misfortune, not poor little Lois's. And of course Minnie's kids didn't get to good schools, because Horace was a socialist; and Andrew has personality problems and Lois is just hopeless: and I got all Peter's insurance money, and my two got a proper education, and now they're on their way to college. They were both born bright and beautiful. I couldn't help it. And I am a widow. Minnie sees that as more of my good luck. I think she hates Horace, really. I loved Peter. That's why I could love Tom. I had a good experience.

To those that hath shall be given; difficult to hand it back, saying I don't deserve this. But that's what I did, Miss Jacobs. That's why I lie here: a corpse in mourning for itself.

Minnie and Horace live in this horrible little house and don't drink, and Tillie's had a stroke and Frank has cancer, and Minnie looks after everyone – and me, I flew First Class out of it all, with Tom. But you can't escape, can you? God stretches out his skinny hand. Minneapolis, the twin city. Minneapolis and St Paul, divided by the river Mississippi, overlapping, interlinked. Tillie and Frank need me to slip them a drink when Minnie's not looking. Lois needs me to keep her on a diet. Andrew needs me to take him to target practice when Horace isn't looking. The only people who don't need me are my kids. They do just fine without me.

I don't know what you think, Miss Jacobs. I don't know which way you want me to be. Where does moral and mental health lie? In looking after yourself, casting off the past, saying I'm well and truly grown-up now; I have a mature, adult, un-neurotic relationship with a totally suitable person: goodbye, family: Minneapolis here I come! Or in saying, well, I'm a person who likes to be liked, who hungers for approval, I'm that kind of person. I accept it, and it's mature and grown-up to say, 'Minnie, count on me. Goodbye, Minneapolis.' Minnie being part of me, however much I rage and scream.

Was what I did an advance into health, or a retreat into unhealthy habit? I have no idea.

I met Tom's family. I played tennis with his brother, bridge with his mother, met the friends, chose the marquee, made out wedding lists. I was the bride from Europe, a little more mature than expected, but okay. I tried not to think of Minnie. They asked me if I had brothers and sisters. I denied her. I said I was an only child. It was my new view of myself. Sooner or later the lie would catch up with me. I didn't care. It was worth it: a holiday, however short, from being twinned, divided, cheated, chained. Rosamund, I said, only daughter of Frank and Tillie, retired general medical practitioners, a couple now living in perfect health and harmony, buoyed up by the respect of the community. They couldn't come over: air travel made Tillie's legs swell up, I said, and Frank wouldn't be separated from his wife. Well, that was true enough. Eternal lovers. The children of lovers are orphans. What did I owe Frank and Tillie? The truth? Why? Who wants women around bringing tales of dissidence and trouble?

You don't approve of this, do you, Miss Jacobs? You don't think people should live by lies. You believe in truth, dignity, self-knowledge, pride. Well, you won. Minnie won. Here I am. The night before the wedding Tom and I walked down by the Mississippi. To the left rose the elegant new towers of Minneapolis outlined in blocks and spires of light: symbols of wealth, aspiration and progress. To the right, across the river, huddled the brooding clutter of St Paul. Unequal twins, growing more unequal day by day. St Paul has the problems: race riots, poverty, squalor. Minneapolis makes sure of that – just heaves them all across the water. If there's a block where the addicts hang out, it bulldozes it flat and builds a shopping mall or a parking lot. A half-moon hung over the river, oddly unsatisfactory as half-moons are. You can't tell if they're waxing or waning. I said as much. Tom pretended not to hear. He liked me to be fanciful, but not too fanciful.
'I'm not going to marry you,' I said.
'Why not?' he asked, when he could find the words.
'Because the moon's not full,' I said. 'If this were a film the moon would be full; not that stupid thing hung up there neither one thing nor the other. I expect it's always like this round here – just plain halved. Minneapolis gets one half, St Paul the other. It will never be right!'

He tried very hard not to hear, but finally he had to. I was not going to marry him. He wept. His parents kept a stiffer upper lip than Frank and Tillie ever managed. He flew me back Club Class. He did not kiss me goodbye. That was the end of it.

Minnie just said, 'Oh, you're back. Made a mess of it for once, did you!' but this I registered as a kind of acknowledgement. And I do the hospital run with Frank and Andrew, and Lois has moved in with me, and we both go round to Minnie's and try to make Horace laugh, and – Miss Jacobs, am I just a fool? Or was this what you wanted for me?

I believe you are asleep: the clicking has stopped. I can hear you snoring; little snores or little sniffs. You might even be crying, for all I know. In pity, or pleasure, or just because there was a half-moon over Minneapolis, catching its skyscrapers in miraculous light, while St Paul lay low, dark and brooding. And it wasn't fair. God makes nothing fair. It is up to us to render it fair.

My fifty-minute hour is up. Your fifty pounds is earned. Thank you for giving me this cancellation. I wonder whom I replaced. And why? Do they have flu? Did they die, or take themselves off unexpectedly to someone more talkative? I have suggested to Minnie that she come along to see you: serve as my replacement on this couch. She says she'll think about it. No. I'm not going out the back door as if you were ashamed of me. I'm going out the front. I don't care whom I meet. I am fed up with etiquette I do not understand. I came in dead, I go out living. As I say, thank you.

Un Crime Maternel

What did they call you? Miss Jacobs? I find that very strange. Only a mother, surely, can understand a mother. What is their purpose in having me see you? If anyone is crazy, it's the law, not me. If it asks for psychiatric reports, which frankly I see as both demeaning to me and damaging to my children, it might at least find someone competent to do the reporting. Or do they have to scrape the barrel for people such as yourself? I don't suppose it's a barrel of laughs, coming here to Holloway and sitting in this horrid little airless green room smelling of cabbage with a locked door and not even a window. In fact the room is rather like the inside of my head used to be before I battered my way out of it, made a hole to let in the air and the light.

Fortunately I can wear my own clothes, being on remand; I don't have to wear their nasty dingy dresses. There isn't an iron available but I keep my skirt beneath my mattress overnight, so the pleats stay in. I like to be smart. I am in the habit of being smart. It's so important to set an example to the children, don't you think? But I suppose you wouldn't know.

Now listen, Miss Jacobs, I will have to make do with you since you're all I have to work with. It is absolutely imperative, do you understand, that you declare me of sound mind. It would do Janet and Harvey no good at all to believe that their mother was insane. It would be too big a burden for them to bear. They are already having to cope with the loss of their father, and Janet's birthday is tomorrow – she will be eight – and she will be disturbed enough that for the first birthday ever I'm not there by her bed when she wakes to say 'Happy birthday, darling.' She may begin to worry, or doubt what she's been told; which is, very sensibly, that I'm on holiday in Greece getting over Peter's death and will be back soon. When I'm out of here I'll be able to talk the whole thing through with the pair of them. It's so important to tell children the truth: if you do, their trust in you is never diminished. Time passes so slowly for children: it is vital that I get back to them as soon as possible: that all this silly and unnecessary fuss comes to an immediate end. They're with Peter's parents, and though Graham and Jenny are not quite as child-centred as I'd like them to be, for people of that generation they're not bad. I can be confident they'll have the sense not to let Janet see the newspapers and of course Harvey isn't reading yet. I used to worry about Harvey's slowness at letters – Janet read at four, and he's already six – but I admit it has its advantages, however unexpected. Crime maternel must be recognized in this country, as crime passionnel is in France. To kill for one's children is no crime: rather, it is something for which a mother should be honoured. I want a medal, Miss Jacobs, not to be had up on a murder charge and remanded without bail for psychiatric reports. I did what it was my duty to do. I chose my children's interests over my husband's interests. Their lives, after all, were just beginning. We do give children this precedence as a matter of course.

It is imperative that I stand trial as a sane person and am properly acquitted, Miss Jacobs, because then the children can deal with it. It may mean moving house and changing schools and names afterwards, of course, but that is nothing compared to the avoidance of trauma. You must see, Miss Jacobs, that I did the only thing I could, in the circumstances I was in.

I had a troubled childhood myself. A father who molested me, a mother who let it happen. I was fostered when I was twelve by a very kind and pleasant family. I know there is good as well as bad in the world. I always wanted to have children, and to give them a perfect life. What is there more important in the world than this? I became a nurse and did well in my profession, but always with my future role as a mother in mind. I am not bad looking, and could, and indeed would, have married on several occasions, but each time I felt the man involved would not make a good enough father. He would have to be loving, kind, genial, patient, intelligent, sensitive to children's needs, and able to provide the proper male authority role within the family group. I began to think I'd never meet the perfect father. I could settle, even happily, for less than perfection for myself, but not for my unborn children!

And finally I met him! Peter! He fulfilled all my requirements, as I did his. He looked for the perfect mother, as I looked for the perfect father. We married, and agreed we would wait a year before starting a family so the children would be born into a settled and secure domestic framework. And that year, I may say, was exceedingly happy. I had always felt, because of my early experience, that sex was not for me. That year with Peter proved me wrong! Then, according to plan, I became pregnant with Janet, and of course after she was born sex became impossible. She could only sleep if she was in the bed with us, and then only if she was at the breast, and I got an ulcer, and you know how it is with small babies. Well, you don't, do you. Let me just say Janet was a sensitive baby, and cried a lot, and then when Harvey came along he turned out to be hyperactive, and I'm sorry to say Peter's views on child-rearing began to change: they simply did not coincide any more with mine.

Does this sound like the tale of a mad woman? I promise you I am not mad.

Peter was teaching at the time, and spent far too much time away from home. I know he had obligations to pupils and college, but he had obligations to his children as well. I insisted that he always be home by bathtime. It is imperative that children have the reassurance that a rock-solid routine provides. But sometimes, on some spurious ground or other, he would be absent. I would have to watch their little faces fall. Splashing about in the water, so important to the development of their tactile responses, their creative drive, just wasn't the same without Daddy. And so he and I began to quarrel. The atmosphere in the home became tense, and that's so very bad for children. They pick up really quickly on vibes.

Peter could, and would, sometimes even in front of them, say terrible things to me. 'Why do you always ask those children questions?' he'd yell. 'Why do you say, "Are you sleepy? Would you like to go in your cot?" Why don't you say, "You do feel sleepy, darling. Now I'm putting you in your cot"?' And of course the answer was so obvious! For one thing, children are not there for the parents' convenience, to be shut up; for another, even with the smallest child it is important to develop consciousness of self. The child knows what it feels; it is up to the parent to decipher those feelings and act upon them. I don't *tell* my child it is hungry: I require it to give me an accurate account of what's going on in its head. That way it learns self-expression. How else? Peter would accuse me of unforgivable things – of over-stimulating the children, of depriving them of pleasure – by which he only meant he'd shut them up if he could by shoving ice lollies in their mouths which would rot their teeth and give them a liking for sweet things which might stay with them all their lives, for all he knew. Or, I'm sorry to say, cared. Please don't think he was a bad father, he wasn't. He loved Janet and Harvey immoderately, and they loved him, which was of course the trouble. I'd feel like tucking them under my arm and running off with them, but how could I? Within two minutes they'd be grizzling and pining for their father.

The upshot of our disagreements over child-care, together with the actuality of those two small lively children, meant I was easily riled and distressed, and spent quite a lot of time in tears which I could not control. Try as I would to be brave and bright for the children's sake, I failed. They would see me red-eyed and depressed, and hear Peter shouting. It couldn't go on. It is the most traumatic and damaging thing for children to hear their parents rowing. Unforgivable to let it happen but it was not my doing. It began to look as if we had to part. Between us we had to provide two loving and caring environments between which Harvey and Janet would travel, since we could not make one. Now I knew I would do my part in this. But I was not convinced he would do his. Already Peter was seeing another woman, a junk-food addict whose idea of an afternoon out with the children was to go to McDonald's on the way to the zoo – can you imagine, a zoo? – the torment of those poor wild caged creatures – and Janet and Harvey actively encouraged to gawp and throw peanuts. Now I'm well aware that it's best for children to see their parents happy, and Peter's sex drive was such that he could only be happy if it was more or less satisfied. I had no grudge whatsoever against his girlfriends, one or all of them, so don't be misled by anyone who says mine was a crime passionnel. It was most definitely – if crime it was – a crime maternel. An act committed for the sake of the children which involves the death and/or disenabling of an incompetent and/or damaging parent. It wasn't Peter's *fault* that this was what he was. Blame God, if you must blame anyone, for creating parents and children whose emotional interests overlap but do not coincide. But there it was. I could see no other way out of an impossible bind.

Divorce, when it comes to it, is so crippling to the child's psyche, is it not? The children suffer appallingly when a family breaks up. Statistics show that a paternal death has a less damaging effect on the children than divorce, so long as the family home is maintained and family income does not fall. So what else could I do, Miss Jacobs? In my children's interests?

I insured Peter's life and he and I, his girlfriend and the children went for a country walk and we picked mushrooms, including a death cap, and I made a beef casserole that evening, and he and she ate it – I am a vegetarian and I never let the children eat beef because of the possibility of mad cow disease but Peter of course would never renounce beef: what he liked he had to have – and it proved as fatal as the books said. Don't worry – I got the pair of them into hospital promptly so the children witnessed nothing nasty. I hadn't realized how suspicious coroners and police can be – I suppose I do tend to think everyone is as child-centred as I am. But this is not insanity, Miss Jacobs, is it? I was doing my best for my children, as the statistics in our society suggest the best to be: and I must get back to them as soon as is humanly possible, for their sake. I presume the court won't be so stupid as not to understand that? What do you think?

A Pattern of Cats

Miss Jacobs, I think our cat Holly is going to die. She has changed the habits of years. Instead of sitting on top of the kitchen dresser, or in the corner between the bookcase and the desk in the living room, she sits in a little patch of grass the other side of the path that runs past our back door. She sits there day and night; she has worn a little dirt nest for herself where no grass grows, fitting her just right: she comes in for meals, but then back she goes. If you try to stop her she squeals and moans. The weather has been so hot and dry for so long, and the nights so warm and full of movement, I thought it was just that – a change in the climate had changed her habits. But last night it rained and there she still sat, in her little muddy nest, pathetic and bedraggled. She complained loudly about it all when she came in for food, but back she went nevertheless, to curl and sit and be dripped upon by delphiniums. What does it mean? I should take her to the vet, but what would I say? This very ordinary tabby cat has changed her habits but otherwise, apart from being a little thin, shows no symptoms of illness? Besides, I'm frightened. Suppose the vet says she has cancer, kidney failure, a tumour? That I must make the decision for Holly as to when she must die? Who am I to make this decision: How did I ever come to be in charge of this small life? It's not the gravity of responsibility you envisage when the little fur-ball of energy first comes bouncing through your door and scrabbles up your velvet curtains, right to the top, leaping and clawing and ruining the surface, and sits on the curtain rail reproaching you, imploring rescue.

That was fifteen years ago, Miss Jacobs. Holly is fifteen, and that's old for a cat, isn't it? Don't you multiply their years by seven for the human equivalent? But that makes her one hundred and five years old, and she certainly isn't that. I'd give her seventy-three in human terms. A neighbour brought her round one morning seventy-three years ago, saying, 'If you don't take in this creature it's the water bucket for her,' so of course we did. We moved over, made room for her. Our proper cat had been run over. There was indeed a vacancy, which we had meant to fill, when the time was right, when our pet-keeping courage was back, with a Persian or a Manx, or something interesting and glamorous. And so we always had the sense about Holly that she'd been foisted upon us; she wasn't quite chosen; she was never a talking point, just Holly the workaday tabby: dismissible stand-in for the proper family cat. Not a nice way to live, though she was always well fed, and wormed, and even stroked when anyone thought about it. I just don't want her to die. It seems important that she shouldn't, this ordinary cat.

I remember that the curtains Holly clawed her way up and ruined that first morning, as I railed against fate and the consequences of my own good nature, were particularly ordinary themselves. It embarrasses me even to think about them. They were of the dusky-rose velvet kind, totally unimaginative. But I daresay they suited the clutter we lived with then; the chaos of books and papers and children's homework, and interesting shells brought back from the beach, and uncleared plates, and the hairdryer on the bookshelf and the football boots left under the table, required a neutral background to sop it up. Jenny was thirteen then, Carl was six. Don and I were forty-something. And Holly was just beginning.

When I first met Don he had a cat called just 'The Cat'. I was jealous of her. She was sleek and black and vaguely Siamese. When I moved in she ran away, and Don was so concerned that I said to him, I remember, 'I suppose you'd rather have the cat than me,' and he looked at me with his clear hard blue eyes and said, 'If I thought too much about it, perhaps I would,' so I never said anything like that again. He would not gratify my neuroses: he would not allow me to whirl up emotional storms. I think that's why I stayed. I was so astonished that someone wouldn't want them, wouldn't exploit them. Jenny was five: she'd had a succession of uncles; once she'd even been kidnapped by the jealous wife of a man I was in love with and had to be rescued by the police – but I told you all about that, Miss Jacobs: we worked that one through – and I knew it was time I stopped that kind of life, the storms and the wonders and the sexual passions, for her sake. Jenny was always the one good thing; her father was the one true love, the one central passion, but he died. I had no cats during those disrupted and illegitimate and wonderful days. They were wonderful. The fifties. I grieve for them. I grieve for them because now we know too much, and then we knew too little, and to know too little is better than to know too much. To be innocent is to be in touch with the infinite and unafraid. And we can never go back to where we were, but must go on, however grievous that may be.

The Cat came back after a week and acquiesced to my presence. She became the proper family cat. She never again slept on Don's bed, but on a cushion I put down for her between the polished anthracite stove and the bookcase. I think she really appreciated the new warm heart of the house. She grew more stolid, even plump. I think she liked the centrally heated core of the bedroom, where Don and I made love; the energy that throbbed out from it and made the houseplants grow and the cakes rise in the oven and gave birth to Carl, and nourished Jenny so she stopped pining and whining and started skipping about. I think The Cat even liked me. She had been presumptuous in her almost human love for Don, and knew it, and was relieved that I had restored some kind of natural balance to the situation. He and I were the masters of the universe, the givers of life; that is to say of Whiskas and a fitting place by the fire. She had no real right to the bed, and felt it. Dogs and cats will sleep on beds if they can, but it makes them feel guilty, and uneasy. In any case they prefer the quiet beds of children or single people: the beds of the young married are too tumultuous, albeit, as I say, life-enhancing; the air in the marital bedroom is too busy for a cat to lie there peacefully for long. The souls of possible children mill around, waiting for permission to enter, to begin, creating a psychic disturbance.

Jenny wasn't happy when Carl was born, but what could we do about that? Carl has his right to life. Jenny came home from school at the age of seven with a diagram of the human reproductive organs and asked if it was true that Don and I had done that to produce this baby and I said yes and she sulked for days. I think some damage was done to her then. Jenny sleeps around a lot, but I don't think she enjoys it much. She enjoys the power she has over men, she says: she enjoys the sense of inevitability, the realization that you don't have to do anything but exist, be anything but what you are, as the male determination takes over, from the first grasping of the arm, the steering of the elbow, out of bars or restaurants towards the bed.

'You must have a low self-image,' I say, 'in that case.'

'I have,' she says.

'I didn't give you one,' I say. 'Don't blame me for that. I spent years telling you how pretty you were, how good you were and this and that, and so you were. And so did Don.'

'He wasn't my real father,' she said.

'Your father was dead or you would have had him.'

'No, you would,' she said, spitefully, leaving me breathless – that was at a time we were still rowing. What can you do? The human situation is at fault, Miss Jacobs. If only men gave birth to girl babies, and women restricted their output to boys, and each suckled offspring of the opposite sex, why then I imagine girls would be as cheerful and confident and positive as boys. They wouldn't have to creep around trying to please, forever looking for the satisfaction that men naturally have; of once having controlled, owned, taken total nourishment from a creature of the opposite sex, and then, loftily, discarded it. Only then, and that will be never.

Sometimes at night The Cat would disturb Don and me. We would be woken by the familiar ghastly caterwauling, the lament of tormented souls. We would go to the window. There The Cat would sit in the back garden in the moonlight, centre of a circle of yowling toms, and when she'd had enough one would move and break the spell and The Cat would split and run, wailing and squealing, and in the morning she'd be on the step, not deigning to use the cat flap, waiting for milk and meat and acknowledgement, bringing with her untold tales of mystery and drastic pleasure.

After Carl was born The Cat had kittens: just the once. The vet said female cats will sometimes do this: some hormone deficiency lowering their fertility; we were lucky, he said. She had two kittens, one black and like herself, one ordinary and tabby. The black, a tom, went to my friend Audrey; the tabby, female, to a friend of a colleague at work, whom I never met, which I daresay was irresponsible, but Carl was teething and I was short of sleep and Don was away and I was having some doomy affair, and you know how things get sometimes. There's no time to do things by the book. Sometimes I wonder if Holly isn't the granddaughter of The Cat. She could be. Holly came from a litter in Audrey's area of London, her father an unknown but black tom: who knows what goes on in the cat world, except that it overlaps and links with ours? Holly and The Cat have the same temperament – broody, impulsive and bad-tempered – and Holly in her youth had a kind of watchfulness which always reminded me of The Cat. Except that The Cat regarded our home as hers by right. Holly is more careful, as if sensitive to being some kind of long-term guest, only allowed in by courtesy. Poor Holly. I should have been more welcoming on that first morning.

The Cat had not a single white hair anywhere: which is, I believe, unusual. Such cats are in demand by witches, someone once told me, searching poor The Cat for evidence till she scratched and ran; which just shows you witches are nutty. Unless, of course, there is some physiological link between the temperament of certain cats and their pigmentation – bearing in mind the fact that, for an unknown reason, a large proportion of all-white cats are born deaf – which means you could rely on an all-black cat to be intelligent, responsive and dependent. In which case anyone who looked to their witchly status would be wise to seek one out. Otherwise, nuts!

Holly, like broody, impulsive and bad-tempered The Cat, is also intelligent, responsive and dependent. When Holly was seven, forty-nine cat years old, I was tempted to bring a kitten into the house. It was the prettiest, liveliest, sweetest little thing. It pranced around, entertaining us; it would jump on my knee as I sat and twirl around and pat my face with a soft paw and then settle and purr. And Holly sat on the top shelf of the dresser and sulked, and she wouldn't eat and she wouldn't drink; and there she sat, glowering and suffering, stiff with jealousy, awkward and plain, and I gave in and gave the kitten to a friend. As with children, as with kittens, the prettiest get adopted first. Holly came down from the shelf and for a day or two attempted to prance and dance and entertain us; she sat on my knee but was too big to twirl and never realized a cat sits comfortably on a human lap only when facing outwards, so she'd slip off and dig her claws in to save herself and I'd scream and it was terrible. Presently, thank God, for it was a most humiliating exercise, she forgot and went back to being her charmless, stolid self, and we all settled down, but I never tried bringing another kitten into the house. We were doomed to Holly.

Jenny was seven when Carl was born. I didn't give Carl away. Carl was an easy, happy, loving baby. I didn't feel the same fierce protectiveness for him that I had towards Jenny, my fatherless child. I don't think I ever clutched Carl to me, the way I did Jenny. I didn't have to. It seems to have done him no harm.

I lament for both Jenny and Carl the fact that they know so much about sex. Sex seems, to them, to have lost the majesty and power it had for my generation. I think they have seen too many pictures, too many films, too much pornography. We only got to see a naked body, and then only a piece of it, in a changing room, or at home, and then by accident. Quickly covered. Our children can name the parts of the body. We could not. There is a word for every activity. We had none. We were moved by instinct, not knowledge. All was dark, and wonderful. For myself and my friends love and sex were another world which ran parallel to the real one. Sex was a secret we hugged to ourselves. There were these two worlds to live in: one in which you could walk on air, in elation, forever unsafe but buoyed up by the knowledge, *he loves me, he loves me and I love him*, sustained by the discovery of undreamed-of pleasures, the excitements of carnal nights, the swooning languor of exhausted mornings in forbidden beds – and the other everyday feet-on-the-ground existence of ordinary practical virtuous life. And you could be two people at once: indeed were two people – even four, for do not the sleeping and the waking life provide us with another doubling? And so we were never bored. At least while love lasted.

Only in adultery, I imagine, does the contemporary young person capture something of this rich duality, quadruplicity, of existence.

The words spoil everything. Penis, vagina, cock, cunt, buggery, fellatio, cunnilingus. How dreary the po-faced responsibility of the sex-education class! Caring relationships! Sensitive approaches! Safe sex. Where is the exultation, the exaltation? Safe sex. Why do it at all, the young must think; absurd, the very notion, that sex might be for pleasure's sake. Perhaps, as with Jenny, it seems okay to do it to exercise power, to improve status, to relieve a low self-image. That's all. Once you define it, you've had it. Language makes nothing of sex. Words should not enter in. But they do, they have, and the world of carnal mystery is denied our children, poor impoverished things; they are obliged to live in their one, unified, seedy, boring, over-real world: no wonder they look so dreary, so hopeless, so alienated, in their black mourning clothes with their white faces, their exhausted eyes. They are mourning a world they do not even know exists.

When Jenny went through her drug phase and nearly killed me with the distress of it, I blamed myself, as you know well, Miss Jacobs. How those first three years, I said, everyone said, must have scarred her! Forget what came after. Poor little Jenny, all her mother Mary's fault, all of it. Mary was irresponsible, said everyone, Mary stayed out, went to parties, drank too much, took a job, had a career even after she married Don and settled down (so-called); Mary was wild, wasn't she; the rows she and Don had; glasses of wine and plates of food flung in restaurants, so what can it have been like for poor little Jenny left at home? The marvel is, said the friends, said the world, said me, that Carl is so steady, not that Jenny went to the bad.

That's what was said, Miss Jacobs, and don't think it didn't hurt me. It did: it gave a new, quite violent dimension to guilt and anxiety and shame. I longed for Jenny to reflect credit on to me, be the proud child of love and sexual freedom, of kindness and cuddles: not this angry skinny devil who shot up heroin and would steal and borrow money from my friends to do it. This laughing buoyant child of the family photograph: Jenny, with her pretty bedroom with the Kate Greenaway wallpaper and the tasteful toys, to come to this? So full of hate, so determined to humiliate her mother? Well, Jenny is okay again. Given up the drug culture, back at college, doing fine: but her twenties thrown away, wasted. Ordinary, loving Jenny back again. But she's almost thirty, and only beginning now. Did she just take longer to grow up than young people are supposed to? Do we have unreasonable expectations, that by the age of twenty a person should be able to cope, go out to work, make a living, live on their own? Perhaps these days the young just take longer to grow up and we must expect them to stay round for thirty years, not twenty? Support them, sustain them, sop up their passions, for all that time; not attempt to pass on to them the burden of responsibility at twenty-five any more than we do when they're ten. It is the much-loved child of the middle classes, Jacob's Benjamin, who so often goes to the dogs, to the drug culture: the Minister's son, the Judge's daughter; see the scandal in the paper? We sneer and say, told you so: a failure in parental love; they were too busy, those bad, bad parents, about the world's business, too little at home; so the child suffered. I am not sure any more it's true: I think there is another element at work here: some other phenomenon. Perhaps the parent-child bond can be too powerful, too immediate; the assumption of love is strong in the parent but quite fails to get through to the child. Too much trust is placed in 'love'. Love is a mere instinct; there is no credit in it; no achievement: no sacrifice. The child demands sacrifice from its parents: not a flow of easy emotion. And does not the child inherit its temperament from both parents, good bits and bad bits alike? The body is not an innately healthy organism which will grow up straight, proud and true unless you somehow thwart it: it is destined to grow up flawed, and as pleasant and perfect, or neither, as the mixture of its parents' genes would suggest. I daresay a mother, or father, can get the best out of that mix or the worst, but you can't make a silk purse out of a sow's ear. Jenny's okay now: and I do think my love, instinctive as it was, helped her, not hindered her. It was not my fault that she took to the dogs: it is to my credit that she survived.

Jenny survived to get to Narcotics Anon, where she met many a child of many a long-lost friend of mine: and they all sit round together, brooding on the sins of their parents, that is to say me, and losing their anger and beginning to laugh.

A strange thing happened, Miss Jacobs. It was how Jenny got out of drugs, got to Narcotics Anon. She was lying on a mattress on the floor of some dreary squat, with black walls and only hate, hate, hate written in white paint on the ceiling for decoration, and she was staring at this ceiling, working out who to con so as to get her next fix, and a black cat jumped on to her chest. A very flat chest, Miss Jacobs, though she's put on some weight since, thank God. It stared at her, and she thought for a moment it was The Cat, but of course it couldn't be, for The Cat was dead.

The Cat had been walking along outside our house when a car went out of control and mounted the pavement and killed her. I watched the spirit go out of her – I held her head as she died. Don was there beside me. We crouched in the street and watched this creature turn from live to dead, from something to nothing, become just a lump of fur. The Cat was twelve. I think she was too proud and stubborn to envisage any kind of lingering death, any diminution of energy: sudden was best for her and worst for us. I don't think Jenny liked the way we grieved. A cat, she said, just a cat. The proper cat for us, we said; the family cat: The Cat, deceased.

But as, years later, Jenny lay on her dirty mattress, a stray black cat jumped on her chest and stared at her for a moment and then ran out of the open door. And Jenny went after the animal to see if it was The Cat though she knew it couldn't be; and once she was out the door in the clear air she began to cry, she didn't know why, and couldn't bear to go back in. Or that's what she told me. Drug addicts are like that: reason drags them down – the hopelessness and pointlessness of existence if you think about it too much – instinct saves them. And one of my friends – I do have friends: I talk so much it saves them the bother of talking: they just hang around: they like it – just happened to be passing and took Jenny in and talked to her and she was receptive, for some reason, and she joined Narcotics Anon, and it worked, though the start was shaky.

Intervention by cat happened on a second occasion, Jenny now tells me. It's why I've come to see you. I need to talk about it. She said she went home one night with a boy she'd met at Narcs Anon. She woke in the morning, before him, full of the guilt and spite that went with her list of one-night stands. She was about to slip out of the bed and slam out of the house. She still had her eyes closed: she was under the quilt. She felt a gentle thud and a scrabble down by her feet and knew a cat had arrived. She felt the cat pick its way up her, over her, sit by her ear. She felt a velvet tapping on her cheek. She opened her eyes and saw Holly staring at her. She lay still. Holly moved across her and tapped about for a bit and circled, and then settled down, purring, between her and the boy. And presently the purr became intermittent and the cat slept, a warm, steady presence. So Jenny felt reassured and went back to sleep too. When she woke, Holly had gone and Saul — that's his name: she's still with him: I really like him: he turns out to be the son of one of my friends — was making coffee in a domestic kind of way, so Jenny stayed. And between them they worked it all out, and neither went back to the needles, which had been in the air.

Now of course it can't have been Holly. Holly lives with us, miles away from Hampstead. But I suppose it could have been some descendant of The Cat's, some second cousin or other of Holly's, which explains the resemblance. I try not to think that Holly did indeed send her spirit out that night, and that is why the poor creature has no energy left and sits in her little nest in the grass outside the house and waits to die, which — and I suppose I must face it — she will soon do. And why Jenny lives, who I thought would die. For ten whole years I dreaded the ring of the telephone which would tell me she was dead.

No, more like something good I once did, once upon a time, just fed back into the pattern of events and worked out okay, and came back to rescue me. Us. Pow! So that phone call never came. Forget the cats. What are cats?

That is all, Miss Jacobs, for today.

The following stories have previously appeared elsewhere: 'Subject to Diary' (*Lear's*, 1989); 'I Do What I Can and I Am What I Am' (*Elle*, 1989); 'The Year of the Green Pudding' (*There's More to Life Than Mr Right*, Piccadilly Press, 1985); 'Ind Aff' (*Observer*, 1988); 'A Visit from Johannesburg' (*Blaubartchen*, Carl Hanser Verlag, 1990); 'Au Pair' (*Honey*, 1985); 'Down the Clinical Disco' (*New Statesman*, 1985); 'Sharon Loves Darren' (*Soho Square*, Bloomsbury, 1988); 'Who Goes Where?' (*Woman*, 1989); 'The Search for Mother Christmas' (*Woman*, 1988); 'A Move to the Country' (*Listener*, 1988); 'Chew You Up and Spit You Out' (*Woman*, 1989); 'The Day the World Came to Somerset' (*Just Women*, 1989); 'A Gentle Tonic Effect' (*Marie Claire*, 1988).

FOR THE BEST IN PAPERBACKS, LOOK FOR THE

In every corner of the world, on every subject under the sun, Penguin represents quality and variety—the very best in publishing today.

For complete information about books available from Penguin—including Pelicans, Puffins, Peregrines, and Penguin Classics—and how to order them, write to us at the appropriate address below. Please note that for copyright reasons the selection of books varies from country to country.

In the United Kingdom: For a complete list of books available from Penguin in the U.K., please write to *Dept E.P., Penguin Books Ltd, Harmondsworth, Middlesex, UB7 0DA.*

In the United States: For a complete list of books available from Penguin in the U.S., please write to *Dept BA, Penguin, Box 120, Bergenfield, New Jersey 07621-0120.*

In Canada: For a complete list of books available from Penguin in Canada, please write to *Penguin Books Canada Ltd, 10 Alcorn Avenue, Suite 300, Toronto, Ontario, Canada M4V 3B2.*

In Australia: For a complete list of books available from Penguin in Australia, please write to the *Marketing Department, Penguin Books Ltd, P.O. Box 257, Ringwood, Victoria 3134.*

In New Zealand: For a complete list of books available from Penguin in New Zealand, please write to the *Marketing Department, Penguin Books (NZ) Ltd, Private Bag, Takapuna, Auckland 9.*

In India: For a complete list of books available from Penguin, please write to *Penguin Overseas Ltd, 706 Eros Apartments, 56 Nehru Place, New Delhi, 110019.*

In Holland: For a complete list of books available from Penguin in Holland, please write to *Penguin Books Nederland B.V., Postbus 195, NL-1380AD Weesp, Netherlands.*

In Germany: For a complete list of books available from Penguin, please write to *Penguin Books Ltd, Friedrichstrasse 10-12, D-6000 Frankfurt Main I, Federal Republic of Germany.*

In Spain: For a complete list of books available from Penguin in Spain, please write to *Longman, Penguin España, Calle San Nicolas 15, E-28013 Madrid, Spain.*

In Japan: For a complete list of books available from Penguin in Japan, please write to *Longman Penguin Japan Co Ltd, Yamaguchi Building, 2-12-9 Kanda Jimbocho, Chiyoda-Ku, Tokyo 101, Japan.*

FOR THE BEST LITERATURE, LOOK FOR THE

☐ THE BOOK AND THE BROTHERHOOD
Iris Murdoch

Many years ago Gerard Hernshaw and his friends banded together to finance a political and philosophical book by a monomaniacal Marxist genius. Now opinions have changed, and support for the book comes at the price of moral indignation; the resulting disagreements lead to passion, hatred, a duel, murder, and a suicide pact.   602 pages   ISBN: 0-14-010470-4

☐ GRAVITY'S RAINBOW
Thomas Pynchon

Thomas Pynchon's classic antihero is Tyrone Slothrop, an American lieutenant in London whose body anticipates German rocket launchings. Surely one of the most important works of fiction produced in the twentieth century, *Gravity's Rainbow* is a complex and awesome novel in the great tradition of James Joyce's *Ulysses*.   768 pages   ISBN: 0-14-010661-8

☐ FIFTH BUSINESS
Robertson Davies

The first novel in the celebrated "Deptford Trilogy," which also includes *The Manticore* and *World of Wonders*, *Fifth Business* stands alone as the story of a rational man who discovers that the marvelous is only another aspect of the real.   266 pages   ISBN: 0-14-004387-X

☐ WHITE NOISE
Don DeLillo

Jack Gladney, a professor of Hitler Studies in Middle America, and his fourth wife, Babette, navigate the usual rocky passages of family life in the television age. Then, their lives are threatened by an "airborne toxic event"—a more urgent and menacing version of the "white noise" of transmissions that typically engulfs them.   326 pages   ISBN: 0-14-007702-2

You can find all these books at your local bookstore, or use this handy coupon for ordering:

Penguin Books By Mail
Dept. BA Box 999
Bergenfield, NJ 07621-0999

Please send me the above title(s). I am enclosing _____ (please add sales tax if appropriate and $1.50 to cover postage and handling). Send check or money order—no CODs. Please allow four weeks for shipping. We cannot ship to post office boxes or addresses outside the USA. *Prices subject to change without notice.*

Ms./Mrs./Mr. _____

Address _____

City/State _____ Zip _____

FOR THE BEST LITERATURE, LOOK FOR THE

☐ **A SPORT OF NATURE**
Nadine Gordimer

Hillela, Nadine Gordimer's "sport of nature," is seductive and intuitively gifted at life. Casting herself adrift from her family at seventeen, she lives among political exiles on an East African beach, marries a black revolutionary, and ultimately plays a heroic role in the overthrow of apartheid.

354 pages   ISBN: 0-14-008470-3

☐ **THE COUNTERLIFE**
Philip Roth

By far Philip Roth's most radical work of fiction, *The Counterlife* is a book of conflicting perspectives and points of view about people living out dreams of renewal and escape. Illuminating these lives is the skeptical, enveloping intelligence of the novelist Nathan Zuckerman, who calculates the price and examines the results of his characters' struggles for a change of personal fortune.

372 pages   ISBN: 0-14-012421-7

☐ **THE MONKEY'S WRENCH**
Primo Levi

Through the mesmerizing tales told by two characters—one, a construction worker/philosopher who has built towers and bridges in India and Alaska; the other, a writer/chemist, rigger of words and molecules—Primo Levi celebrates the joys of work and the art of storytelling.

174 pages   ISBN: 0-14-010357-0

☐ **IRONWEED**
William Kennedy

"Riding up the winding road of Saint Agnes Cemetery in the back of the rattling old truck, Francis Phelan became aware that the dead, even more than the living, settled down in neighborhoods." So begins William Kennedy's Pulitzer-Prize winning novel about an ex-ballplayer, part-time gravedigger, and full-time drunk, whose return to the haunts of his youth arouses the ghosts of his past and present.   228 pages   ISBN: 0-14-007020-6

☐ **THE COMEDIANS**
Graham Greene

Set in Haiti under Duvalier's dictatorship, *The Comedians* is a story about the committed and the uncommitted. Actors with no control over their destiny, they play their parts in the foreground; experience love affairs rather than love; have enthusiasms but not faith; and if they die, they die like Mr. Jones, by accident.

288 pages   ISBN: 0-14-002766-1

FOR THE BEST LITERATURE, LOOK FOR THE 🐧

☐ **HERZOG**
Saul Bellow

Winner of the National Book Award, *Herzog* is the imaginative and critically acclaimed story of Moses Herzog: joker, moaner, cuckhold, charmer, and truly an Everyman for our time.

342 pages   ISBN: 0-14-007270-5

☐ **FOOLS OF FORTUNE**
William Trevor

The deeply affecting story of two cousins—one English, one Irish—brought together and then torn apart by the tide of Anglo-Irish hatred, *Fools of Fortune* presents a profound symbol of the tragic entanglements of England and Ireland in this century. *240 pages   ISBN: 0-14-006982-8*

☐ **THE SONGLINES**
Bruce Chatwin

Venturing into the desolate land of Outback Australia—along timeless paths, and among fortune hunters, redneck Australians, racist policemen, and mysterious Aboriginal holy men—Bruce Chatwin discovers a wondrous vision of man's place in the world. *296 pages   ISBN: 0-14-009429-6*

☐ **THE GUIDE: A NOVEL**
R. K. Narayan

Raju was once India's most corrupt tourist guide; now, after a peasant mistakes him for a holy man, he gradually begins to play the part. His succeeds so well that God himself intervenes to put Raju's new holiness to the test.

220 pages   ISBN: 0-14-011926-4

FOR THE BEST LITERATURE, LOOK FOR THE

☐ **THE LAST SONG OF MANUEL SENDERO**
Ariel Dorfman

In an unnamed country, in a time that might be now, the son of Manuel Sendero refuses to be born, beginning a revolution where generations of the future wait for a world without victims or oppressors.

464 pages   ISBN: 0-14-008896-2

☐ **THE BOOK OF LAUGHTER AND FORGETTING**
Milan Kundera

In this collection of stories and sketches, Kundera addresses themes including sex and love, poetry and music, sadness and the power of laughter. *"The Book of Laughter and Forgetting* calls itself a novel," writes John Leonard of *The New York Times*, "although it is part fairly tale, part literary criticism, part political tract, part musicology, part autobiography. It can call itself whatever it wants to, because the whole is genius."

240 pages   ISBN: 0-14-009693-0

☐ **TIRRA LIRRA BY THE RIVER**
Jessica Anderson

Winner of the Miles Franklin Award, Australia's most prestigious literary prize, *Tirra Lirra by the River* is the story of a woman's seventy-year search for the place where she truly belongs. Nora Porteous's series of escapes takes her from a small Australia town to the suburbs of Sydney to London, where she seems finally to become the woman she always wanted to be.

142 pages   ISBN: 0-14-006945-3

☐ **LOVE UNKNOWN**
A. N. Wilson

In their sweetly wild youth, Monica, Belinda, and Richeldis shared a bachelor-girl flat and became friends for life. Now, twenty years later, A. N. Wilson charts the intersecting lives of the three women through the perilous waters of love, marriage, and adultery in this wry and moving modern comedy of manners.

202 pages   ISBN: 0-14-010190-X

☐ **THE WELL**
Elizabeth Jolley

Against the stark beauty of the Australian farmlands, Elizabeth Jolley portrays an eccentric, affectionate relationship between the two women—Hester, a lonely spinster, and Katherine, a young orphan. Their pleasant, satisfyingly simple life is nearly perfect until a dark stranger invades their world in a most horrifying way.

176 pages   ISBN: 0-14-008901-2